COOKIE!

...and the MOST MYSTERIOUS
MYSTERY in the WORLD

COOKIE

Developed by Konnie Huq and James Kay

First published in Great Britain in 2021 by
PICCADILLY PRESS
4th Floor, Victoria House, Bloomsbury Square, London WC1B 4DA
Owned by Bonnier Books
Sveavägen 56, Stockholm, Sweden
www.piccadillypress.co.uk

This is a work of fiction. Names, places, events and incidents are either
the products of the author's imagination or used fictitiously.
Any resemblance to actual persons, living or dead,
is purely coincidental.

A CIP catalogue record for this book is available
from the British Library.

ISBN: 978-1-84812-989-4
also available as an ebook and audio

1

Typeset by Perfect Bound Ltd
Printed and bound in Great Britain by Clays Ltd, Elcograf S.p.A.

Piccadilly Press is an imprint of Bonnier Books UK
www.bonnierbooks.co.uk

CHAPTER 1

Secrets

Why is it that parents always say 'nothing' when you ask them questions about their conversations with other grown-ups?

It's like they think we're being nosey or that we're too young to understand things. But how can we

learn anything if they don't tell us stuff in the first place?

In general, a good

way to learn things is to ask questions, but 'nothing' is NOT a helpful answer!

I suppose there are a few exceptions . . .

What is two minus two?

What is the opposite of everything?

What is gnihton backwards?

What is the meaning of life?

Today, my mum got a letter from my nani (her mum) and spent a good twenty minutes reading it and laughing out loud, like it was the funniest joke book ever written. When I asked her what it said, she just kept saying 'nothing'.

ha ha · hee hee · ho ho

'*Nothing* doesn't make people laugh,' I said, to which she replied, 'Really, it's nothing . . . just Nani being Nani.' Well, that's even more ridiculous! Of course Nani is being Nani. Who else would she be? Father Christmas?! Now *that* would be weird.

Nani, is that you?

Ho ho ho . . . merry Xmas!

I think saying 'Nani is

COOKIE!

...and the MOST MYSTERIOUS
MYSTERY in the WORLD

WRITTEN and
ILLUSTRATED by

KONNIE
HUQ

Piccadilly
PRESS

just being Nani' is a tautology. A tautology is when you repeat something that's already been implied in the same sentence, like 'the scorching sun was boiling hot'. Well, of course it was, otherwise it wouldn't be scorching!

Or calling a mystery mysterious . . .

Mysterious mystery? That's a tautology. Of course mysteries are mysterious, duh! This book must be rubbish if the author doesn't even know that!

Unlike most other people at school who see their grans all the time, I hardly know my nani cos she lives in Bangladesh. I've only been there once, and although it was for the whole of the summer holidays I was just a baby so I don't remember it.

Wish I could speak Bengali . . . wish I could speak English too, for that matter!

Goo goo ga ga!

'Nani' is the Bengali word for a gran who's your mum's mum. Your grandparents from each side of the family are called a different thing. Keziah always laughs at the fact that a 'Nana' is a man and a 'Dadi' is a woman, but it's actually pronounced 'Nunna' and 'Duddy'.

Nani: granny
that's your mum's mum

Nana: your mum's dad

Dada: your dad's dad

Dadi: your dad's mum

My nani lives in a small village in Bangladesh. She doesn't even have Skype or a mobile phone, so every now and then she sends Mum these really long letters updating her on the family back home and all the village goings-on. Judging by the amount that my mum laughs, Nani seems to be funnier than a stand-up comedian.

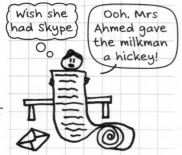

Wish she had Skype

Ooh, Mrs Ahmed gave the milkman a hickey!

Maybe if Nani lived here she *could* be a stand-up comedian. I like to think I've inherited her genetics and that I'm quite funny too.

Genetics are the coding handed down to us from our biological parents that give us our inherited characteristics.

Nani, here's some flowers

How kind! You get that from your mother

Nani, Cookie's being annoying

Oh dear. She gets that from her father!

Talking of coding, Bengali's a bit like a code. After Mum had finished Nani's letter, she left it on the kitchen counter. I tried to have a look, but it was like a foreign language to me . . . probably because it is, I guess. Bengali looks really cool written down. It all hangs off a line and is in neat shapes. I already know how to write my name . . .

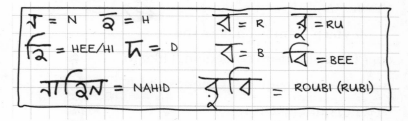

My sisters can write their names as well – we worked it out from this Bengali alphabet book Mum bought us.

I was only a few months old when we went to Bangladesh, but my sisters came back speaking Bengali really well and now it's like everyone in my family can speak in code except for me.

My eldest sister, Nahid, speaks it better than my middle sister, Roubi. I can hardly speak it at all – I only know three words.

But I like to think they're three really important words . . .

Clement Boudin in our year at school can speak FOUR languages.

1. French – he was born in France and his parents are French.

2. English – he moved to England in Year Two and picked up English within a few months.

3. Spanish – his childminder only spoke to him in Spanish, so he learnt it from her.

4. Russian – yep, Russian!! His mum's parents are Russian and they taught it to him.

He could be an interpreter and work for MI5!

Imagine speaking FOUR languages! How cool is that?! Apparently, babies can learn hundreds of different languages . . .

Agent Boudin reporting to MI5: I have the target in my sights. She wants water . . .

Each language uses only about 40 sounds or 'phonemes', which distinguish one language from another. At birth the baby brain has an unusual gift: it can tell the difference between all 800 possible sounds. This means that infants can learn any language they're exposed to . . .

Can you repeat that in French for me? I prefer speaking French at home

Merci!

I decide to bike over to Keziah's. I love having my new bike – it's so brilliant being able to see Keziah whenever I like.

Where's she going this late? It's 3 a.m.!

As I'm leaving the house, Jake, who lives next door, is finishing off washing his mum's car and decides to tag along.

'Hey, Jake!' I say. 'How come you're washing the car again? You only just did it last week!'

'Mum keeps making excuses to get me out of the house,' he explains. 'Not only have I washed the car twice today, but I've also mown the lawn AND been to the shops three times to pick things up for her. It's so odd. She'll probably be over the moon that I'm going to Keziah's with you. She's acting SO weird and being really mysterious.'

Mum . . . ? Is that you?

'Let me guess,' I say. 'When you try to get to the bottom of it, she just says it's "nothing", right?'

'Right!' he replies.

Why are parents so complicated sometimes? Why all the secrecy? We're old enough to be trusted with stuff at our age.

Blah, blah, blah . . . That's what a flexible mortgage is. Happy now?

zzzzzzz

At Keziah's, her dads, Mal and Paul, are having a few people over to watch the football on the telly. They're laughing lots and keep talking about 'that time under the bleachers at their local football club'.

The three of us head up to Keziah's bedroom.

'What are bleachers?' I ask.

'It's an American word,' says Jake. 'They're the seats that are tiered or raised in rows, like stairs.'

'I know that, but I'm still none the wiser as to what happened under them.' Keziah sighs. 'It was before I was born so I have no idea what they're talking about.'

Keziah's room is in the loft, so it has sloping ceilings – it's a bit like being in a secret hideaway in the roof. It's also got massive skylights, which you can look out of and nosey at the whole street undetected! It's really cool and good for spying.

Keziah loves drawing and her whole room is covered in artwork – in fact, the whole house is! Paul and Mal have framed her pictures and hung them everywhere and some of them look really professional.

'Heyyy! Look what I've got,' says Jake, pulling a brand-new Z-Box 3 Pro out of his backpack.

'No way! You don't even like gaming! How come you've got one of those?' I ask, trying to hide my jealousy. I love gaming but can only dream of owning my own Z-Box 3 Pro.

'I know, right?' says Jake. 'My mum got it for me out of the blue and I've no idea why. She keeps getting me presents.'

We start to formulate theories behind Jake's mum's sudden generosity, secrecy and general weirdness. Keziah reckons she might have an online gambling habit.

'She probably needs you out of the house so she can go on the laptop and log on to the cyber casino without you knowing,' she says.

'But why all the gifts?' asks Jake.

'Maybe she buys you stuff with her winnings out of guilt,' I chip in.

'Not a bad explanation,' he replies. 'Although it doesn't explain why she's being extra nice to me.'

'Maybe she's trying to make up for the fact that your dad's moved out?' suggests Keziah.

I wonder what Jake's mum's hiding. Keziah is brilliant at keeping secrets. I would trust her with my life.

She's almost *too* good at it. One time, Axel Kahn told her that he'd seen Mr Hastings, our deputy head, and Miss Rai, one of the reception teachers, in Nando's together sitting in the corner behind a pillar!

Keziah didn't even tell *me* cos Axel made her promise not to tell anyone. Not even ME?!! Come on, Keziah!! I've no idea why it was such a big deal in the first place. Two teachers eating chicken . . . hardly a classified state secret.

Agent Boudin here. The targets are in Nando's

I only found out when Axel accidentally mentioned it to me. Anyway, if it *was* supposed to be a secret, why go somewhere as popular as Nando's?

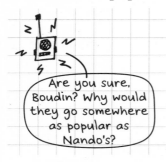

Are you sure, Boudin? Why would they go somewhere as popular as Nando's?

But the point is . . . KEZIAH DIDN'T TELL ME!! She said it was because Axel made her swear on her life. I was really annoyed. I think she's learnt her lesson – we tell each other everything now.

I made her tell me a secret then she collapsed

I made her swear on her life not to tell!

Does make you wonder, though . . . was it some sort of staff meeting or is something else going on? What did they chat about? School? Teaching methods? Their undying love for each other?

My eldest sister, Nahid, is the WORST at keeping secrets. There was the time when she

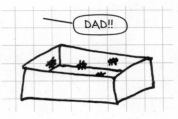

told Dad about my secret woodlouse farm, which I kept in a shoe box under my bed . . .

AND the time she told Mum I'd stolen a cola

bottle from the pick and mix . . .

AND the time she told Mum AND Dad that I pretended my cardigan was a pet cat . . .

After we finish playing on the Z-Box, Keziah shows us how to make a coding wheel.

A coding wheel is basically two circles of card with the alphabet written on them, and you set the circles so that each letter of the alphabet corresponds to a totally different letter. You can then code messages to send to each other.

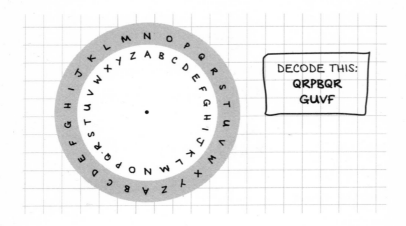

DECODE THIS:
QRPBQR
GUVF

We all decide to make one, and we code and decode messages until it's time to go home.

When I get back, there's an ambulance parked outside my house. What on earth is going on? My dad and Roubi are standing on the pavement and a few other neighbours are gathered around too, including Jake's mum.

The ambulance drives off. Huh?

'What's going on?' I ask

'Get in the car,' says Dad. 'Your sister's been in an accident. We need to go to the hospital.'

CHAPTER 2

Coding

Nahid had been on her way home from uni and, just as she was crossing the road, she got run over right outside our house. In the car, Dad tells me that it was a hit-and-run. What a cowardly driver – fleeing the scene of the crime like that!

Poor Nahid. The police even turned up to take statements,

but unfortunately there were no witnesses. Roubi said that *her* friend's dad got hit by a car once and fractured his tibia (a bone in the leg). It was so badly broken that they had to put pins in each half of the broken bone and connect them up with rods on the outside. This meant he had metal inside AND outside his leg. He must be, like, one-fiftieth cyborg!

PIE CHART OF COMPOSITION

$\frac{1}{50}$th cyborg
$\frac{1}{50} = \frac{2}{100} = 2\%$

$\frac{49}{50}$th dad
$\frac{49}{50} = \frac{98}{100} = 98\%$

He bleeps every time he goes through airport security now . . .

Bleep!

Do you have any metal on you?

On me?! I have metal **in** me!

On the way to the hospital, it feels like everything takes ages. The roads are really busy, and every traffic light seems to be red.

STOP!!

When we finally get there, we have to wait for someone to free up a parking space. Then Dad complains that the car park is really expensive . . .

PARKING CHARGES

1 hour: £500
1 minute: £10
1 second: 18p

Annoyingly, he doesn't have enough change so we have to wait for another ten years until someone comes along who can swap him some for a note.

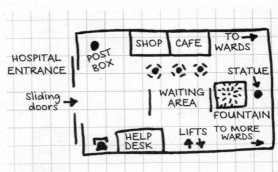

Excuse me, can you swap a £50 note for 250 twenty-pence pieces, please?

250 twenty ps? That'll only get you an hour in here!

When we eventually get inside, the hospital is busy and bustling like a mini town

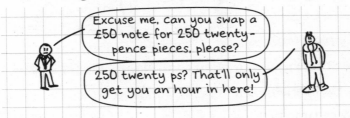

HOSPITAL ENTRANCE
POST BOX
SHOP
CAFE
TO WARDS
STATUE
Sliding doors →
WAITING AREA
FOUNTAIN
HELP DESK
LIFTS
TO MORE WARDS

centre. There's a post box, a cafe, a newsagent's and people everywhere. There's even a small fountain with a statue next to it.

We head to the cafe while we wait to find out from Mum which ward Nahid will be in after they've done her X-rays.

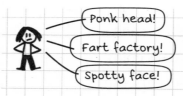

I think of all the times I've argued with her or been mean to her . . .

I'm SO sorry about all of that, Nahid. Please forgive me! Will she be OK? Could she have broken a bone? Did she hit her head? Will she even recognise me?

What happens if she has to have surgery? Or if she's in a coma? Or they have to turn off her life-support machine?!

Roubi hasn't stopped talking since we left the
house – talking about anything and everything.
Maybe this is her coping
mechanism. Meanwhile,
I've zoned out and Dad's
being very quiet, so she's
just talking to herself,
really.

I hate waiting and not
knowing what's going on. This
is so terrible. I just didn't see it
coming.

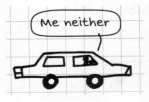

I look around at the people wandering about
everywhere . . . doctors, nurses, visitors, patients.
Some in dressing gowns, some with stethoscopes,
others buying flowers for loved ones,
but all with one thing in common . . .
the gift of life. Precious life. Please can
Nahid be OK?

'Was there a lot of blood?' I finally ask, feeling
my own blood draining from my face. I glance up
to see a motionless patient being wheeled along in
a bed attached to a drip. Not very helpful right now
as I fear the worst . . .

'No blood,' says
Dad. 'She's going to be
absolutely fine.'

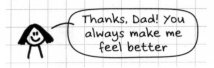

'Unless there was internal bleeding that we
couldn't see,' says
Roubi.

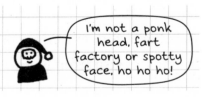

'I doubt it,' says
Dad. 'She was in good spirits in the ambulance.
Hardly someone on the brink of death.'

Oh. All that worrying for nothing. It's just as well,
as I was definitely
in the right in most
of our arguments.

After what
seems like another year, we go up to see Nahid on
her ward. She's in bed but acting totally normal –
the same as ever, really. Nahid just being Nahid.

What was I expecting?
Father Christmas?!
Now *that* would be
weird.

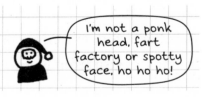

She laughs at me and Roubi
overdoing it on the hand sanitiser from
the wall dispenser. It splots on the floor.

SPLOT!

20

'It's free.' She chuckles. 'Fill your boots!'

Excuse me, that'll be £59 for the hand sanitiser — we're charging now to help fund the NHS. The car park fees aren't making enough!

The doctor tells us that Nahid has cracked her pelvis (a bone in the hip) but that she's going to be as right as rain.

I'm always right — it's going to be rainy later!

'She'll be on crutches for a while,' she explains. 'But apart from that she'll be fine. She'll stay in hospital for one night, then be discharged tomorrow.'

All that unnecessary worry. Nahid can be such a drama queen sometimes.

Wish everyone would stop fussing around me and go home — it's nearly time for *EastEnders!*

Later that evening at dinner Mum announces that Nani is coming to visit from Bangladesh.

'I was going to surprise everyone,' she says, 'and tell you all together when Nahid was home for the weekend, but that hasn't exactly worked out, has it?! Poor girl. I think she's had enough drama for one day, so I'll tell her tomorrow!'

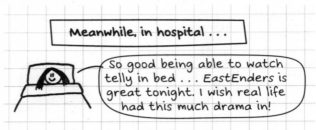

Amazing news! And great timing too! Mum will now be staying with Nahid for a few days at her halls of residence to help her get used to her crutches. This means Nani will be looking after us while Dad is at work!

Look after us?! Yay!! Grannies are always real softies. She'll probably be extra lenient as she lives thousands of miles away so she never usually gets to see us.

This is going to be GREAT. Dad has an Indian restaurant and is often there till closing time, which means that Nani will be supervising a lot of bedtimes. Woohoo!!!! Roll on late nights, laughing at her hilarious jokes and munching on junk food!

Brilliant! Exciting times ahead . . .

The next day at school flies by. We're currently
doing a class topic of computers and coding and
we've been learning about the Enigma coding
machine. I like the word 'enigma'. It means a puzzle
or a mystery.

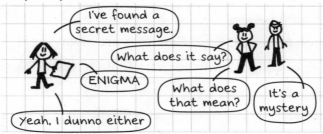

In the Second World War, the Germans used
the Enigma machine
(which basically looks
like a typewriter) to
send coded messages
to each other.

It was used to send secret information with details of military tactics and operations.

The British government got a team of very clever people together, including Alan Turing, the father of modern computer science, to work as code-breakers and decipher the German messages. They worked at a place called Bletchley Park and developed Colossus, the world's first programmable digital electronic computer, which managed to decode a load of the messages.

Thanks to their work, the Second World War was shortened by two to four years, saving 14 million lives.

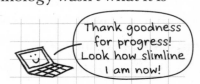

Back in the 1940s, technology wasn't what it is today, so Colossus took up a whole room.

So fascinating.

After we learn about the Enigma machine, Mrs Chen hands out some worksheets with codes on them for us to crack. The first few are easy . . .

8	5	12	12	15
H	E	L	L	O

A = 1   B = 2   C = 3   D = 4
E = 5   F = 6   G = 7   H = 8

She thought it would be funny to have messages like 'I decoded this sentence and all I got was this lousy message' and 'Mrs Chen is my favourite teacher ever.' She *isn't*, but that's a whole other story . . .

Mrs Chen would be incredibly easy to miss in a crowd – she's so meek and mild. It's like she's not even there half the time.

I guess the messages *are* quite funny for her. Pretty creative, really. People often think that if you're sciencey you can't be arty and vice versa. I disagree. I think you can be both. For instance, it's pretty creative to come up with the Enigma machine!

25

Come to think of it, if you tip Chen over the edge she changes from meek and mild to angry and terrifying. Plus, she can be pretty creative with her punishments when she's cross. It's very rare, though – I've only ever seen her do it once.

COUNT OUT ALL THE IRON FILINGS IN THIS JAR NOW!!

The last code on the worksheet is quite a tricky one because the sentence is really long. As everyone is busy working it out, Mrs Chen hands out leaflets for an exhibition at the Science Museum on the history of computing. It gives free entry to any child accompanied by a paying adult. *This* I wanna go to. I tuck the leaflet safely away in my bag.

THE SCIENCE MUSEUM PRESENTS . . .
Full details overleaf
THE HISTORY OF COMPUTING
✳ FREE ENTRY WITH PAYING ADULT ✳

It takes a good ten minutes before anyone can work out the code, but eventually Tina Mories cracks it. Code-breaking Tina?! Who knew?!

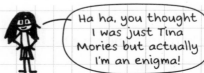

Ha ha, you thought I was just Tina Mories but actually I'm an enigma!

It's the end of the lesson and the rest of us are still none the wiser, so Mrs Chen tells us to take the puzzle away to decipher at home. For those who don't manage it, we'll be told the answer tomorrow at registration. Apparently, it's a pretty important message. Tina's not allowed to tell anyone. Important? Huh?! What could it be?

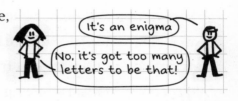

What?!! The school is being closed down by the authorities

On our way home, Jake and I wonder out loud what the message could be.

It's an enigma

No, it's got too many letters to be that!

We bump into Tayo Akinola and his big brother, DJ, at the green. The green is a big patch of grass that lots of secondary-school kids hang out on.

The green

DJ and his friends are often there listening to music or skateboarding. They're SO cool. DJ is into street dance and Jake has seen some of his videos on YouTube and says he's really good.

YouTube

Wot's up YouTube . . . don't forget to subscribe and hit that Like button

0.0 / 27.00

Channel MCDJ

Tayo says hi and DJ offers us some Doritos. WOW!! DJ is actually speaking to us!! And not only that but he's offering us Doritos!!!

Hmm . . . these crisps are past their sell-by date – I'll give them to those kids

After we head off we are on a high! DJ knows who we are!! Wow!!

Wonder who those kids I gave my crisps to are?!

Hmm . . . I wonder what DJ stands for? Maybe it's an abbreviation and his actual name is Deejay? There's a Vijay in our school.

I'm VJ

Or is it because he's an actual DJ?

Or is DJ short for something like

Daniel James?

Daniel James Akinola.

Daniel!

Just call me DJ, Mum, it's better for my image

Or maybe it stands for two words to describe him, like 'Dangerously Jubilant'.

I'm the bomb!

Or 'Downright Jealous' . . .

TOP 100 PEOPLE THAT ARE THE BOMB

Wish I was the bomb . . . it's NOT FAIR!

28

Or maybe it stands for a longer name or a foreign one, like the way I'm nicknamed Cookie because people find my Bangladeshi name a bit of a mouthful.

Maybe he's shortened a longer Nigerian name, as his dad's Nigerian? Diarachukwundu Jideofor?

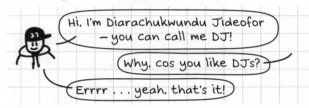

Either way, DJ is really sound.

We walk home all pleased with ourselves after our brush with the cool kids. Once I'm in the house, I race upstairs to start code-breaking.

After jiggling the letters about, I finally manage to work it out. You have to put the first thirteen letters in a row and then the next thirteen letters in another row directly underneath. This makes it pretty easy to work out the solution . . . so A=N and N=A. B=O and O=B. I then realise I could have just used the code wheel . . . DUH!!!

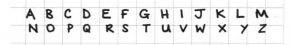

A	B	C	D	E	F	G	H	I	J	K	L	M
N	O	P	Q	R	S	T	U	V	W	X	Y	Z

The message reads . . .

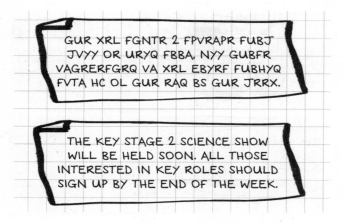

GUR XRL FGNTR 2 FPVRAPR FUBJ JVYY OR URYQ FBBA. NYY GUBFR VAGRERFGRQ VA XRL EBYRF FUBHYQ FVTA HC OL GUR RAQ BS GUR JRRX.

THE KEY STAGE 2 SCIENCE SHOW WILL BE HELD SOON. ALL THOSE INTERESTED IN KEY ROLES SHOULD SIGN UP BY THE END OF THE WEEK.

OMG!! A science show?! I wonder if we'll have to audition?! *I'd* be interested in a key role! This is SO exciting!!!!

CHAPTER 3

Woodburn High

Since Nahid got back from hospital she's been bossing me around even more than usual.

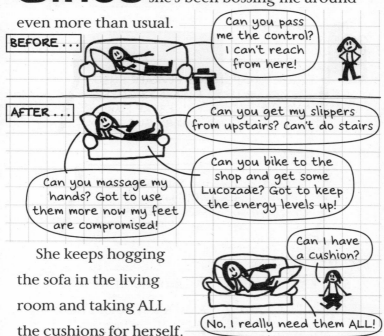

BEFORE...

Can you pass me the control? I can't reach from here!

AFTER...

Can you get my slippers from upstairs? Can't do stairs

Can you bike to the shop and get some Lucozade? Got to keep the energy levels up!

Can you massage my hands? Got to use them more now my feet are compromised!

Can I have a cushion?

No, I really need them ALL!

She keeps hogging the sofa in the living room and taking ALL the cushions for herself.

Meanwhile, we all have to watch what she wants on TV . . .

Hello and welcome to Celebrity Match-Up Adventure Island Extreme

She's watching this show called *Celebrity Match-up Adventure Island Extreme*, where a bunch of famous people are marooned on a desert island and have to pair off and eat bowls of snail poo and witchetty grubs and do really gross things to survive . . .

But who would want to eat poo?

You get to be on TV!

One celeb pair had to make themselves clothes out of leaves and sticks. They then had to live together for a week away from the others. They stayed in a tree pod made of dung and reeds that their teammates had built for them.

Can't believe the tree pod didn't collapse in the rain storm last night

Can't believe they're still alive. Must stink up there!

We need to make a weaker tree pod next time — they'll win at this rate!

The island pairs are only allowed to eat meals if they get on with each other, so often they just pretend they do to get fed. The more they get on, the better their meals, which range from worms to sirloin steak and chips.

Funny thing is, my sister spends more time chatting about the show with her friends on social media than actually watching it!

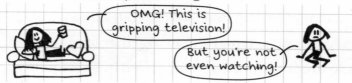

Her and her uni friends have made a group chat about #CMUAIE (short for *Celebrity Match-up Adventure Island Extreme*). They constantly message each other while it's on, so she's always sniggering away over all the crucial bits.

Not that I'm getting

drawn in to the show or anything . . .

Most evenings, Roubi is in her bedroom doing her homework or reading a book, and because Dad is often at the restaurant and Mum has been busy sorting out the spare room for Nani's visit, I'm the only one having to endure everything Nahid watches on the telly.

Anyhow, Mum and Dad are totally indulging Nahid, and Roubi and I are getting a tad fed up with it.

Worse still, she keeps eating all the snacks in the house.

People from her uni have been sending her cards and flowers and she's even had some chocolates.

Hmmmm . . . this breaking your pelvis thing has its advantages.

Advantages of breaking your pelvis:

1. Gifts

2. Sofa-hogging

3. Being waited on hand and foot

Disadvantages of breaking your pelvis:

1. Can't do sport (though she doesn't do much anyway, so not really applicable)

2. Requires crutches to get around (though she is on the sofa most of the time now, so not really applicable)

3. Stairs are tricky (though she makes me get her everything from upstairs now, so not really applicable)

It's fun trying to use her crutches, though. When we were waiting for her to be discharged from hospital, Roubi and I kept nicking them to see who could get about on them the fastest.

Come back! I need the loo!

Ask for a bedpan — I'm doing a timed lap!

I wish she'd got a cast and then we could have doodled and written on it.

I went to hospital and all I got was this lousy cast

Casts are getting rarer and rarer these days. Priti Prashad in the other year group didn't even get a cast when she broke her ankle. She got a special boot thing instead, so it was easier to have a bath and sleep and stuff.

You can write stuff on me

You can wash with me so you won't smell

Oh yeah! Good point . . .

But Roubi's friend's dad (the one who bleeps when he goes through airport security) had a full cast and had to slide a ruler down the side of it to scratch his leg. They'd often get stuck . . . he lost about three rulers in that cast!

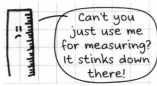

Can't you just use me for measuring? It stinks down there!

Casts can get really smelly as you can't wash them. Worse still, you can't even remove them yourself – you have to have them sawn off when you're better.

Scary . . .

My mum cracked her rib sneezing once. It was so weird. She was in the kitchen one day, chopping onions, and she sneezed really hard, and her rib really hurt afterwards. Turns out she had actually managed to fracture it just by sneezing. Can you believe it?!

I don't remember Mum hogging the sofa and

being waited on. Business as usual for her . . . washing, cleaning, cooking, drop off, pick up.

Did you know:

- Iguanas sneeze more than any other animal!!!

- You can't sneeze in your sleep.

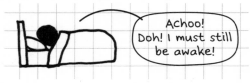

- Sneezes are an important part of the immune system, ridding the body of bacteria and viruses through the nose. You can expel 100,000 germs in a single sneeze.

- You *can* sneeze with your eyes open – it's a myth that your eyeballs will pop out!

- Sternutation is another word for sneezing.

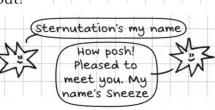

The next day at school, Mrs Chen reveals the coded message about the science show. Only about a third of the class managed (or even bothered!) to crack it.

Meh . . . Mrs Chen will tell us the answer tomorrow if it's such an important message

Ever since I can remember, our school has put on an annual science show. Sometimes there are science-based comedy sketches, sometimes there are little drama reconstructions of the inventions of important things, and one year there was even an amazing bubble display.

Did you know that the biggest bubble ever blown was 50 metres long and 60 cm in diameter?

Hooray! Let's celebrate with some bubbly!

Often, of course, there are just lots of cool experiments and demonstrations done live on stage.

Mrs Chen explains to us that some of the

Next up on this year's science show, let's see what happens when we add this minty sweet to a fizzy drink . . .

Oh no–not again!

secondary-school kids will be helping us to put it

on. That should be cool. Keziah heard Mr Hastings telling the school secretary in the office that he thinks the science show is a silly idea and we're over-stretching school resources by putting it on when the school's Christmas production is coming up at the end of term. He was really ranting about it!

We only just had a science competition

He said that the Ofsted school inspection is due soon and he reckons it could even be this term. If we don't get graded well, I bet he'll blame the science show!!

Ofsted failed us!

I blame the science show

Mr Hastings is renowned for having 'good days' when he's as nice as pie and 'bad days' when he's on the war path. This was definitely one of his bad days! Maybe he had an argument with Miss Rai, the reception teacher from behind the pillar at Nando's. Tee-hee!

I wanted peri-peri, not vusa! This is too hot! I'm leaving!

Come back! I'm sorry!

On the way home from school, the big kids are all hanging out on the green again. Tayo says DJ is going to help organise the science show, which is really cool, as he knows who I am now. After all, he gave me one of his Doritos! Hopefully this will mean I get a decent role.

When I signed up to take part in the science show, I noticed the board was already pretty full. Top of the list was code-breaker extraordinaire Tina Mories, who managed to find out about it first. Tina's parents are both computer programmers – no wonder she's such a whizz!

Tayo points out a tall girl sitting on a bench nearby, and he mentions that she'll also be helping to organise the show.

'That's Vicky Chen,' he says. 'Her mum is none other than our science teacher, Mrs Chen!'

She must *really* be into science.

Mrs Chen is tiny, but Vicky is pretty tall. Vicky's dad must be a giant . . .

. . . although facially you can definitely see the family resemblance.

Heading home, I feel excited, and even more so when I see an airport taxi driving away from our house. Airport?!! That can only mean one thing . . . NANI IS HERE!!!! YAY!!!!

CHAPTER 4

Nani

When I get in, Nani is in the kitchen wearing about three jumpers AND a puffer jacket. She's chuckling away with Mum in Bengali.

Poor Nani thinks the UK is freezing because Bangladesh is so hot in comparison. It doesn't help that it's not even summer over here. I wish I could understand what they're saying, but I can't. So annoying. Nani looks just like an older, wrinklier version of my mum. Maybe I'll look like her one day too!

When she sees me, she hugs me tightly for about three hours, saying stuff in Bengali that I can't understand.

Nani smells of coconut oil and has a friendly, leathery face. She looks pretty ancient, which is fair enough as my mum has six brothers and sisters. Who wouldn't look old after having that many kids?!

In Bangladesh, it's normal for people from my mum's generation to have loads of brothers and sisters. My mum's cousin has thirteen brothers and sisters and there are people with even more than that!

The Guinness World Record holder with the most children is a Russian lady who has sixty-nine! Sixty-nine??!!!! That's more people than in the whole of Year Five!

Hopefully Nani will tell me stories about what Mum was like when she was my age. I wonder whether she was like me.

This daughter of mine is scruffier than I expected. Maybe I'll luck out with my grandchildren!

Nani has brought us a load of presents from friends and family in Bangladesh. It's mainly clothes, as well as a strange assortment of food. You're not supposed to bring food or drink into the country from Bangladesh without declaring it to the customs officers first.

CUSTOMS

Anything to declare?

আ?

Oh . . . never mind!

Mum and Nani are laughing away at her smuggling antics – they reckon she would make a very capable cross-border smuggler. She seems so innocent and harmless. No one would ever suspect her of having millions of pounds' worth of diamonds in her shoes!

These shoes are uncomfy!

Among other things, she's brought:

- lots of jars of mango pickle made by an auntie who is apparently renowned for her mango pickle!
- strange-looking veg that are hard to get over here and are all wrapped up in Bangladeshi newspaper.

45

- loads of bags of what looks like a cross between crisps and Bombay mix.

Most of the clothes she's brought over are traditional Bangladeshi dress.

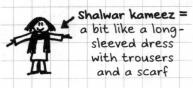

Shalwar kameez = a bit like a long-sleeved dress with trousers and a scarf

I run up to Roubi's room to give her presents to her, but she's not in there so I leave them on the bed. When I go back down, Nani isn't in the kitchen any more. Mum says she's gone for a lie-down in her room. What?! But she only just got here! I haven't had a chance to get acquainted with her yet. It's only four o'clock in the afternoon!! A bit early for sleeping, if you ask me!

Twit twoo . . . What's wrong with sleeping in the daytime?!

Mum assures me there'll be plenty of time to hang out with Nani. In fact, tomorrow Mum will be dropping Nahid off at uni, so we'll get to spend lots of time together when Dad goes to work at the restaurant. And you never know . . . maybe she's just having a catnap and she'll resurface for dinner.

Zzzzzz

I hope so. It would be handy to have Mum here, as my lack of Bengali skills means I'll need an interpreter.

By the time it gets to dinner, Nani is still having 'a lie-down', or rather she's in a deep sleep. Mum says she's got jetlag, which means her body clock's been disrupted because she's travelled so fast across different time zones.

Due to the rotation of the earth around the sun, it's night-time in Australia when it's daytime here. It's the same for other countries that are on opposite sides of the globe from one another.

International time zones measure the time according to where you are on the earth so that everyone has daylight during the day and darkness at night. When it's midday in the UK it's also 7 a.m. in New York, 5 p.m. in Bangladesh and 10 p.m. in Sydney.

UK
12.00
midday

New
York
7 a.m.

Bangladesh
5 p.m.

Sydney
10 p.m.

Countries to the west of us are further ahead in their day and countries to the east are further behind.

G'day . . . although us Australians are down under, time-wise we're way ahead of you

I decide to talk loudly outside Nani's room, hoping she'll wake up, but it doesn't work.

I peek round the door and see that she's breathing heavily, smiling away mid-slumber. She sighs contentedly and I sidle up to her bedside and try shouting . . .

'NANI'S FAST ASLEEP!!!' I yell, right by her ear, like I'm reporting back to my parents.

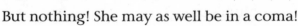

But nothing! She may as well be in a coma!

Just as I'm leaving her room, she rolls over on her side, mumbles something in Bengali and starts some gruff low-level snoring.

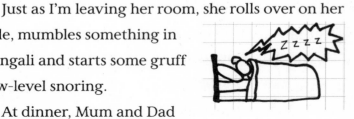

At dinner, Mum and Dad

put Auntie's mango pickle on everything they eat and chomp away happily, complimenting it as though they're in a five-star restaurant.

If you're in a pickle when making dinner — try me!

They act as if it's some sort of magic sauce that has the ability to transform all food into gourmet dining!!

Dad doesn't usually have dinner with us, but he's going to the restaurant a bit later than usual tonight, so we can all have a 'welcome to the UK' dinner together in Nani's honour! Well, that's backfired slightly, hasn't it?!

I wonder whether that annoying son-in-law has gone to the restaurant yet, or should I keep pretending to be asleep?

Roubi and I try some mango pickle. Euggghhh! It's tart!!

Who are you calling tart?

I love mango and I love pickle, but this stuff?! No, thanks! Nahid tries some too and makes out like it tastes good! Yeah, whatever, she's just trying to act all grown-up.

She's sophisticated!

Mango is usually my favourite fruit. It's so good in all forms . . . except Bangladeshi pickle!

My top-three mango tips:

- Mango coulis (pronounced coolie). Often seen on dessert menus. A liquidised mango sauce, great on vanilla ice cream, cheesecake and other simple puddings.

Mango coulis

- Solero – my favourite ever ice lolly. Although it's supposed to be a blend of exotic fruits (peach, passion fruit, pineapple and mango), it tastes completely mango-y to me. Has an outer shell of exotic fruit ice lolly with an inner core of ice cream. What's not to love? Yum!

Mango lolly

- Mango hedgehog. The easiest, non-drippiest way to eat mango.

Scored with knife

Mango

Mango hedgehog

I actually planted a mango stone in a plant pot a couple of years ago and now we have a mini mango tree in the corner of our living room. It doesn't bear fruit yet, but it looks pretty cool. I call it Mangy. It's about 40 cm tall and is a bit like a bonsai palm tree!

Hi, I'm Mangy!

After dinner, Nani is STILL ASLEEP!!! She's had over four hours' sleep and it's not even night-time yet! Unbelievable!!!

I watch *Celebrity Match-up Adventure Island Extreme* with Nahid. I'll actually quite miss our viewing sessions when she goes back to uni tomorrow.

Hmm ... Cookie secretly likes that show!

One of the celeb pairings have to eat grubs and locusts before abseiling down a ravine. It's their first meal in days. The lady throws up and the man looks so hungry it almost seems like he wants to eat her sick or something. So gross.

Yum

The sick on my rope is making it slippery. Hope we don't fall!

Tomorrow, I'll just watch TV with Nani instead. Finally, we can go back to watching normal stuff.

You secretly like that show

TV is a really good way to learn a language. Maybe I can learn Bengali while Nani learns English.

With KFC's new bargain bucket you get 3 extra sides

Nani's English is getting really good now

On the way home from school the next day, Jake is complaining about his mum.

'She's acting even weirder now,' he says. 'She's joined this book club and she doesn't even *read* books. Plus, she's bought me *another* game for my console!'

'Poor you,' I reply sarcastically, 'getting all those presents for doing absolutely nothing.'

Jake's quite into gaming now, so at least some good is coming from all this. Since making our coding wheels, we've written loads of messages to each other, which we hold up at the windows at the sides of our houses, as they face each other. It's kind of fun. Half the time we end up opening our

windows and just yelling to each other when we can't decipher the messages!

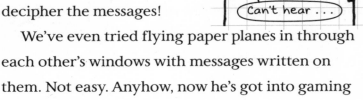

We've even tried flying paper planes in through each other's windows with messages written on them. Not easy. Anyhow, now he's got into gaming again, the novelty seems to have worn off a bit.

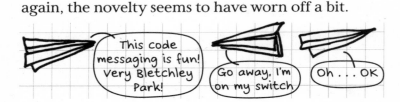

When I get home, Nani is asleep on the sofa! So much for all the fun we were going to have together with my parents out of the way. Great. I've just managed to shift one sofa hog back to uni in time for another one to move in!

Next time I'll take all the cushions! And maybe later I'll watch CMUAIE . . . yeah!

I'm really starving, so I open a bag of the Bombay mix crisp things. They're actually pretty good. I wonder if I can fly one across to Jake via paper aeroplane through his window. It's a spectacular fail.

Gravity's pull > My throwing force

We try to send aeroplane messages back and forth for all of five minutes before he decides that *Super Mario* is way more fun than me. Charming.

Can you jump over giant coins and double in size?

No

Well then!

I decide to start playing some video games on our Z-Box 2. Although it's a little old, it's pretty much mine now. It was originally Nahid's, but she's grown out of it and is off at uni, and Roubi's not as into gaming as I am. I crank up the volume . . . but

Nani is still asleep on the sofa, totally oblivious.

This sofa is SO comfy. I should just stay here instead of in the spare room

Huh?! There's a new high score on *Khushi's Quest* since the last time I played a couple of nights ago. It's my favourite game and I'm the only one who ever plays it. Really odd.

KHUSHI'S QUEST
NEW HIGH SCORE
580999

Huh?!

Roubi and I get bored of waiting for Nani to wake up, so we eat the food Mum has left us for dinner. After we're done, Nani is STILL asleep so we both stay up really late!! Woo-hoo!! At about 11.30 p.m., we hear chuckling from the living room and peer down through the banisters to see Nani watching a late-night repeat of *CMUAIE*! What the heck?!! Nani is turning into Nahid!!! First sofa-hogging and now watching trash TV. What next?!

I suppose they do share the same genetics . . . but so do I. Sometimes I think I'm adopted!

Mum and Dad, is there any chance I'm not related to you?

In our dreams . . .

We hear a car door bang shut outside and run back into our bedrooms, thinking Dad is back. I dive into my bed and pull the duvet up over my head but don't hear Dad's keys in the front door. Hang on . . . it's too early for him to be back. I look out of the window to investigate and spot Jake's mum walking up to their front door, grinning away to herself.

Well, book club has ended late tonight . . . it's nearly midnight!!! And that's when I notice . . . there is NO BOOK in her hand . . .

Oh dear! I left my book at book club

She clearly hasn't been to book club. Where on earth has she been?!

CHAPTER 5

Vicky Chen

A car starts up and drives off. Hmmm. Jake's mum has been dropped home by a stranger and it definitely ISN'T a taxi driver. I can tell by the way she turns, blows a kiss (!), waves, walks up the path, then turns back and blows ANOTHER kiss (!!!!!) before disappearing off inside the house.

Why did I just blow a kiss to Marjorie from book club?!

I can see that Jake's bedroom light is turned off, so he'll be oblivious to all this drama. It might be worth his while quizzing his mum on the book she was meant to be reading for this so-called 'book club'. I'm quite sure this tactic would unravel her story pretty quickly . . .

So, Valerie . . . tell me about the existential underlying message in the narrative

Huh?!

Luckily for Jake, though, I manage to note down the make and number plate of the car, as well as the fact that there's a small dent in the back bumper.

Well, I say number plate, but actually I mean half the number plate. The other half is obscured due to the angle I'm leaning against the window at . . .

Man, this is really squashing my nose

I'm already craning really hard to see properly. My neck is at the maximum extension possible without permanently injuring it.

I knew that was a mistake!

Although I can't make out the car's colour in the dark, I notice that it has a sticker on the back windscreen, a bit like one of those 'Baby on Board' stickers.

BABY ON BOARD

I can't quite see what it says, though . . .

BOOK CLUB MEMBER ON BOARD

I jot down all the info in my diary. When I say 'diary', it always starts out being a diary at the beginning of the year. For the whole of January, it pretty much is a diary and I write in it every day, but then around February the entries start getting more scant. In March there are even fewer and

by April I've pretty much stopped using it altogether and it becomes a notepad!

I always think at the beginning of each year that this will be the year when I actually write in it consistently, all the way through to December. I really mean it at the time, but then it just doesn't

happen! I've even tried to 'back write' it before, where I go back and try to fill in the gaps that I missed, but it never really works . . .

It's not even the type of diary where you write 'Dear Diary' followed by all the stuff that's

happened in a day. It's the week-per-page type – more for writing appointments and 'random happenings' in . . .

. . . but even then I still can't manage it!

Mum says it's like when Dad buys a new 'toy'. He uses it for the first week and then the excitement

slowly wears off and eventually he forgets it even exists. Like the time he got a bread maker . . .

Week 1 – fresh bread every day. Bread maker lives on kitchen counter.

Week 2 – fresh bread every other day. Bread maker now lives in the kitchen cupboard.

Week 3 – fresh bread only once. Bread maker lives in the cupboard under the stairs.

We eat too much bread anyway

Before you know it – supermarket bread. Bread maker lives in the attic.

At school the next day, I can hardly keep my eyes open. I ended up going to sleep really late. I even heard Dad coming in. That was well past midnight. He and Nani were downstairs chortling away for ages, which kept me up even later. I really need to break the ice with her.

I know we'd have a laugh, but so far it's been pure boredom. She's either been fast asleep or watching telly, and when I try chatting to her she just smiles at me blankly and I feel like I'm bothering her. Totally annoying that the grown-ups find her so hilarious. Even Roubi and Nahid chat with her in Bengali. I'm the only one who can't.

At break time, I start to tell Keziah all about Jake's mum, but I've decided not to mention it to Jake yet. I don't want him jumping to any conclusions. I could be wrong, after all. Maybe his mum just left her book-club book in the car by accident?

And maybe she was late back as everyone decided to have a meal after book club to discuss the book more?

There could be so many explanations for why his mum is acting weird . . .

And this week's book club book is . . .

How to Act Weird

It can't be easy bringing up four kids, including a toddler, when your husband has moved out and lives on the other side of town. Maybe she's got a second job as a waitress or something to earn a bit of extra money?

But would she *really* blow a kiss to a book-club buddy or a work colleague? To be fair, she probably would. She's really warm and friendly. It was more of a casual kiss-blow that turned into a wave than pure kiss-blowing, if that makes sense?!

Casual kiss-blow [kazh-oo-uhl kisbloh]
Half kiss, half blow with a bit of a wave thrown in for good measure.

Pure kiss-blow [pyoor kisbloh]
Very definite kiss and blow with the hand directing the kiss towards the recipient.

I guess that's not *too* weird a thing to do to a friend. My mind is racing now. I just want to get to the bottom of why Jake's mum is acting so strangely, but I'll have to tread carefully.

As I'm filling Keziah in, Jake comes over.

'What are you guys chatting about so intensely?' he asks.

'Uhhhh . . . nothing!' I say quickly and very guiltily, as though I've just been caught stealing the Crown Jewels from the Tower of London.

Nothing?! What a hypocrite?! I sound just like my mum. I feel myself looking uneasy. Why can I not keep a calm head in these situations, like Keziah?

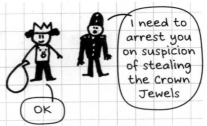

'We were just discussing ideas for the science show,' says Keziah quickly. 'You got any?'

'Yeah,' I add. 'What do you reckon to "Notivity"?!'

I came up with the title last night while I was trying to get to sleep. As it's NOT a nativity play like lots of schools do every year, I thought 'Notivity' would be a funny title. It could be all about evolution, which is the scientific theory first put forward by Charles Darwin that humans evolved from apes.

 Jake and Keziah laugh.

After school, when we get to the science show meeting in Mrs Chen's classroom, everyone is milling around and chattering away. The big kids are sitting at the back of the room and Mrs Chen is at the front trying to shush everyone. It isn't working.

She outlines a few basics, explaining what the show needs to be about, but it falls on deaf ears. After five minutes or so she gives up.

'Er, OK, all . . .' she splutters, blushing apologetically, something she often does when speaking in lessons. 'I'll hand over to the senior-school students. They'll take it from here . . . errr . . . OK. Thank you. Bye.' She slips out of the door, looking relieved to be making a swift exit.

With that, Vicky Chen bounds to the front of the class with an air of confidence and utter coolness.

'Hi, I'm Vicky, head of the senior-school drama club,' she booms and everyone instantly looks up and quietens down. She gestures towards her friends, including DJ, who are all sitting on tables at the back of the room.

'The rest of the gang and I are going to help you guys put on the show of a lifetime!'

She grins an infectious grin that injects a shot of excitement into the room.

Vicky is nothing like her mum. The phrase 'like mother, like daughter' was not invented to describe *them*, that's for sure.

She commands the group with ease, and she seems so cool that it makes you want her to like you.

We go around the room discussing ideas for the show. I'm eager to please. I like the company of older people. They're so much more mature and appreciate the finer things in life, like my knowing about Darwinism.

I suggest my Notivity idea. Vicky smiles with perfect teeth and perfect dimples and says, 'That's great! Very funny!' I beam with pride. Vicky Chen likes MY idea! These people are *definitely* my tribe. I like Vicky.

DJ laughs too. 'Notivity! Nice one, Cookie!'

Even better!! Now everyone knows that *he* knows who *I* am. SO COOL! If I play my cards right, I'll be instrumental in helping to put this show on. Apart from Vicky (who is the daughter of a science teacher, after all), I reckon I'm into science way more than most people in this room. *This* could be my big moment.

CHAPTER 6

Not Notivity

I feel a real sense of pride as Vicky writes 'NOTIVITY' in capitals on the whiteboard and underlines it.

'OK, guys! Any more ideas?' she asks, scanning the room.

NOTIVITY

Several hands shoot up, including Suzie Ashby's. I can see she is visibly annoyed that Vicky likes and, better still, is *using* my title.

It was probably also a blow to her that DJ knew my name. This all gives me a secret sense of satisfaction. Vicky surveys the show

Isn't it spelled nativity?

of hands – everyone is desperate to be picked. Including me.

'Cookie,' she says, pointing straight at me. Wow, this just gets better and better!

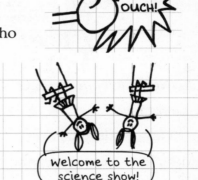

'Well, maybe we could start the show with the story of how we evolved?' I suggest.

'Errrrrr . . . not very grabby, is it?' replies Vicky without hesitating. This is like a punch in the face.

Now Suzie's the one who looks secretly satisfied. Grabby?! This is a science show, not the Cirque du Soleil . . .

Anyhow, *I* think it *is* pretty grabby that we ALL originated from primates and before that simpler mammals and before that reptiles and before that sponge things and before that probably plankton.

plankton	sponges	reptiles	primates
1.5 billion years ago	750 m years ago	320 m years ago	55 m years ago

We've come a long way since 4.1 billion years ago, when the earliest life forms first appeared.

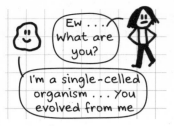

'I know!' shouts out Suzie. 'Alison and I could cartwheel in from opposite sides of the stage!'

'You can *both* do that?' says Vicky excitedly. 'Great idea!'

Now, Suzie and Alison both look like the cat who got the cream.

What on earth has cartwheeling got to do with science?!

This is bonkers!

'We could make it part of a whole opening sequence to kick the show off with a bang!' adds Suzie.

Average speed of cartwheel

$= \dfrac{\text{distance travelled}}{\text{time taken}}$

$= \dfrac{260 \text{ cm}}{4 \text{ seconds}}$

$= 65 \text{ cm per second}$

'Love it!' squeals Vicky, high-fiving Suzie.

'But what have cartwheels got to do with science?!' I ask, frustrated.

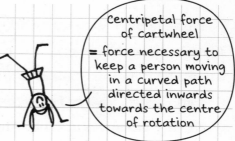

'How about we make it like an American cheerleading routine?' says DJ, before bursting into a chant. 'Gimme an S, S! Gimme an I, I! Gimme an N, N! Gimme a C, C! Gimme an E, E! What have you got? And then everyone can shout out, "Science!!"'

'That's brilliant, Deej!' grins Vicky. 'We could even use pom-poms!'

I seem to be the only one who's noticed that he's spelled 'science' wrong.

'It's still not very sciencey,' I say.

'Good point, Cookie,' replies Vicky.

I smile smugly.

'Ooh, I know!' she shouts. 'Everyone can wear lab coats!'

Lab coats?! Seriously?!

I look over at Jake but even *he* seems into the idea . . . I guess he does love dancing.

'Fab!' beams Vicky. 'That's the opening sorted.'

Next, Vicky gives us all half an hour to work on something to perform in the main body of the show. Meanwhile, she giggles away with the rest of her secondary-school gang at the back of the room and they all start looking at pictures and stuff on their phones.

She makes it quite clear that, first and foremost, our acts need to be entertaining and that we can add in the science bit later!

'My mum can help with the science part,' she says.

Turns out Vicky is way less like Mrs Chen than I could have ever imagined!! She's not into science

AT ALL! She reckons she's more of an 'arts' person, and acting is 'her thing' . . .

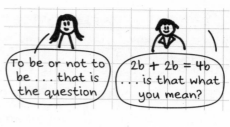

. . . which is why she's head of the drama club!

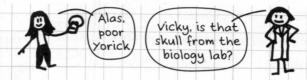

Personally, I've always felt like I'm an arts *and* science person. I adore drama, but I love maths and science too. I reckon the two go hand in hand more and more these days. Loads of Hollywood films have amazing CGI (computer-generated imagery) and, similarly, video games have brilliant creative artwork in them – they're almost life-like!

Keziah and I decide to do our section for the show on Ada Lovelace, who I once read about in a book on inspirational women. She lived in the 1800s and her dad was Lord Byron, the famous poet (arty), but her mum was a mathematician (sciencey).

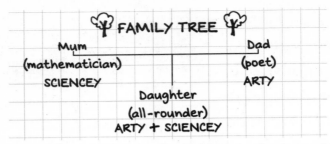

FAMILY TREE

Mum
(mathematician)
SCIENCEY

Dad
(poet)
ARTY

Daughter
(all-rounder)
ARTY **+** SCIENCEY

Ada worked with Charles Babbage, who invented the computer. Whereas he saw computers as pure number-crunchers, like calculators, she realised that they had the potential to do all kinds of things, like draw pictures, make music and so much more.

She totally nailed it and foresaw how we use computers and programming today in modern society. What a woman!!

After performing our epic tribute to this formidable lady in front of the whole group, Vicky merely says, 'Hmmm . . . I'm not sure it's quite right for the show.'

She then goes on to praise literally EVERYBODY ELSE for their offerings, most of which resemble acts on a talent show, NOT informative and educational pieces for a *science* show.

Meanwhile, Alison and Suzie do more cartwheels and throw in a load of handstands too, plus some other gymnastic bits and pieces. Jake does a really good

dance number, and DJ shows him a couple of street-dance moves. Then somehow it all descends into chaos, with everyone busting out their dance moves. Before I know it, the whole thing has turned into a flossing and dabbing contest!

A pinging noise interrupts my thoughts. DJ, or 'Deej' as everyone seems to be calling him now, has received a news text alert on his phone that Molly has walked off

Celebrity Match-up Adventure Island Extreme. Breaking news alert?!! Seriously?!! News?!

After that, the senior-school kids are straight back on their phones updating each other on the gossip.

Before the meeting finishes Vicky announces which acts everyone will be doing in the show. It's a bit like being on *Britain's Got Talent*, only on an episode in which Keziah and I have got four red crosses!

Keziah's relieved that our act hasn't made the cut and offers to do props and stage management instead. Performing in front of an audience is her worst nightmare.

74

Great. Now I have nothing to do. The only science enthusiast CUT from the science show!

They've even forgotten to give me a new role. From 'Notivity' to 'Not-Even-In-It-Tivity'.

As we're all leaving, I tell Vicky that I need a new role. Uh-oh . . . she's probably gonna say I can be Suzie's and Alison's assistant or something hideous like that. Right now they appear to be the stars of the whole show and Vicky seems quite taken with them.

I feel sick.

'You can be in Jake's dance sequence if you're up for it?' says Vicky.

Phew. That's actually worked out way better than I thought it would. I have a decent enough part and I'll be with Jake. Only one problem, though . . . I'm rubbish at dancing, especially compared to him, and I'm definitely not stage-worthy!! This I'll have to work on . . .

After rehearsals, Jake is walking to his dad's in the same direction as Keziah, so I say goodbye to them both and decide to take a shortcut home the other way through the car park.

As I weave my way in and out of the cars, I hear Mrs Chen's voice.

'Seriously, Martin, failing a driving test isn't the end of the world! I failed my chemistry GCSE the first time and look where I am now!'

'Yes, Janice, but you didn't fail SEVEN times!' replies Mr Hastings.

Chen Hastings Cookie

Seven times?! He must be the world's worst driver!! And Mrs Chen failed *chemistry*?!! Maybe she *is* Vicky's mum after all!!

Keziah, Jake and I have recently taken to passing coded notes back and forth in class to amuse ourselves and pass the time. This is the perfect bit of info to put in one of them! I duck down behind a car so as not to be seen earwigging, but then I hear a voice behind me, which makes me jump.

'Cookie! What are you doing down there?'

I look up to see Vicky Chen grinning down at me.

'Errr, dropped these!' I say quickly, dangling my house keys in the air.

'Phew! I thought you were wanting to hang out with my mum and discuss Ada Lovelace or something!' she teases.

Well, I hope it was teasing and not making fun of me. She bounds off. 'Mum, can I have a lift home?'

I get up from the ground and scuttle off in the other direction, brushing gravel dust off my uniform. Can't wait to pass notes in class tomorrow!

The next day at registration, everyone is restless. Mrs Mannan seems miles away, as though she doesn't even care. I whisper to Jake, Keziah and Axel that I've got some good goss.

'As long as it's not about *CMUAIE*,' laughs Jake.

'Certainly not!' I exclaim in mock outrage.

'Is it about what happened under the bleachers that time?' Keziah grins.

'Nope,' I say.

'Hastings and Rai?' suggests Axel.

'You'll see,' I reply as we all sit down. I start scrawling down my juicy piece of gossip in cipher using A=N on our code wheels.

UNFGVATF
SNVYRQ UVF
QEVIAT GRFG
FRIRA GVZRF

I pass the note about and the others unscramble it with ease.

'No way!' whispers Jake. 'Dunno which is worse, Chen and chemistry or Hastings and driving!'

Keziah and Axel are both giggling. Mrs Mannan looks up and clocks the note right away.

'If that note is so funny, then we really should share it with the whole class, shouldn't we? Bring it here!' she demands.

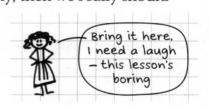

Bring it here, I need a laugh – this lesson's boring

Keziah reluctantly hands the note over to Mrs Mannan. Oh great. She's gonna make her read it out and then it'll be the green seats or detention for all of us. It's bad enough passing notes in class and giggling, but when the note is about not one, but two, of your colleagues and their miserable failings, that isn't ideal.

Uh-oh. We're in for it now. This is NOT good.

CHAPTER 7

Mysterious Flowers

'This should be interesting!' says Mrs Mannan, clearing her throat and putting on her reading glasses.

Suzie Ashby and Alison Denbigh start sniggering on the other side of the classroom. I'm not sure whether Mrs Mannan actually knows it was me who passed the note to Keziah in the first place. Maybe Keziah could say she found it on the floor or something to save me from being implicated?

Miss, it just fell out of the sky into my hands. Dunno how it got there!

hee hee!   ha ha!   hmpf!

Suzie and Alison are still giggling.

'Maybe *you'd* like to read it out, Suzie, since this is all so amusing to you?' says Mrs Mannan.

That wipes the
smirk off Suzie's and
Alison's faces instantly.

hmpf!   hmpf!   ha ha
                hee hee!

Suzie gets up
reluctantly and makes her
way to the front of the
classroom, her bunches
sashaying back and forth
in a smug, irritating
manner as she walks.

How can bunches be irritating and smug?

To be fair, we are on Suzie's head

True!

Mrs Mannan passes the paper to
Suzie. I sink down in my seat, realising
that I've written the note in purple
ink. I'm probably the only person in
the class with a purple ink pen!

Sorry!

I found it down the back of a radiator at home.
Nahid said it was hers from a couple
of years ago and that I could keep it.
At the time I couldn't believe my luck
at this instant win, but now it will be
my downfall.

Sorry again!

Suzie takes the note from Mrs Mannan, looks at
it and scrunches up her face, confused.

'I can't read it, miss,' she says.

'Stop being impertinent, Suzie, and read it out now,' demands Mrs Mannan.

'But I can't!' she protests.

'One way or another we're all about to find out what it says, so please save us the bother and share it with everyone,' Mrs Mannan retorts. 'This isn't reception class – you know how to read!'

Not so sure she does!

'But it makes no sense!' whines Suzie.

'Why were you laughing?' replies Mannan.

'I didn't write it!' protests Suzie, exasperated.

'So why were you laughing?' snaps Mannan.

Suzie looks blank and then, thinking on her feet, blurts out, 'Because Tayo farted!'

'I didn't fart!' cries Tayo.

The whole class is laughing now.

'He did!' pipes up Alison, supporting her friend.

What . . . ? How have I got embroiled in all this?!

'Didn't!' Tayo insists.

The laughing continues. This diversion is good. Maybe the note will be forgotten about.

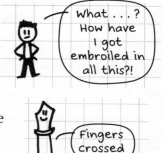

Fingers crossed

'Sit down, Suzie, I'll read it,'

snaps Mrs Mannan, grabbing the note off her.

On second thoughts, maybe it won't be . . .

She looks at the crumpled paper and frowns. 'Who wrote this?'

Silence.

The situation doesn't seem to be defusing at all, so I decide to own up before my purple pen gives me away and I get into even more trouble.

'I wrote it,' I mumble.

'Very commendable of you to own up, Cookie,' replies Mrs Mannan. 'Now speak up and tell us all what it says!'

I pause and try to think of something to say. 'Well . . . it's just a jumble of letters, really. You see, I was testing out my new purple ink cartridge,' I explain. 'It's not even a note, actually, more of a sample . . . Like a tester to see

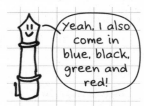

what the ink looked like. You
know, the way you can see
paint samples in B&Q before
you paint a wall?'

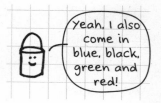

'That's quite enough, thank you, Cookie,' says
Mrs Mannan sternly. 'I know what a sample is.'
She screws up the paper and tosses it in the bin.

'We've wasted more than enough of this lesson
already, thank you. Please do
your pen-testing in your own
time. Right, class, turn to page
fifty-seven of your textbooks.'

Thank goodness the message had been written
with the code wheel and thank
goodness none of the others had
decoded the message on the same
piece of paper. *That* was a close call.

Later that day, we have a lesson about coding
and programming with Mrs Chen. Tina Mories,
it would seem, is something of a
coding whizz. Not only the secret
alphabet/hidden messages kind,
but the computer kind too.

We have to make this animated car drive to the shops, and then add lots of other actions along the way, like stopping to get petrol . . .

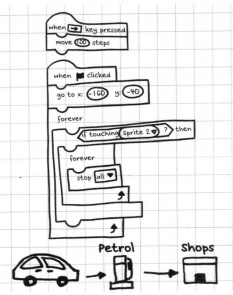

. . . and driving to the vets to pick up the dog.

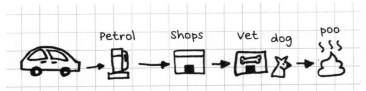

Each time we redo the exercise it gets a bit more complicated, but Tina can literally do the whole thing in her sleep.

Finished . . . z z z

She's like some kind of tech genius.

I'm also good at formulating passwords that are hard to crack, changing aspect ratios of TVs and doing factory resets on all sorts of tech

Apparently, this is how all programming works: by inputting a set of instructions for the computer to follow.

In no time at all, Tina is way ahead of the rest of us. Even Mrs Chen is impressed and tells her she's so good that she should take the class!

Tina says her dad got her into computers at a really young age.

Watching my little animated car drive around, I wonder whether Mr Hastings is going to take his driving test for an eighth time! He must be horrific on the road . . .

As for Mrs Chen failing chemistry, how did she manage to get a job as a science teacher!? She must have lied in job interviews and faked her grades on her CV or something.

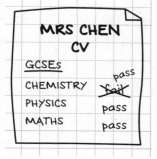

I mean, how on earth will the school be awarded Outstanding status at the next inspection with teaching staff like this?! We'll be lucky to scrape a Requires Improvement at this rate!

It all makes sense now . . . Vicky Chen being bad at science isn't so strange after all.

Ugh, that reminds me . . . Jake and I need to come up with a dance routine to show her at next week's science show rehearsals.

On the way home from school, Jake starts trying to teach me dance moves for the show.

'Everything is counted in bars of eight,' he says, 'so let's practise by doing arm moves first and we can add the legs in later.'

'Uh . . . OK,' I say.

I feel a bit self-conscious hand-clapping and jiving as we walk down the road.

Jake's moves are fluid and seamless compared to mine, but after a while I start to get the hang of it. As long as you remember the order of stuff, it's actually quite fun.

Hope people see us!

It's actually VERY FUN. I think I like this dancing lark. We start singing an Aliana Tiny track that is currently number one in the charts while doing the arm moves in time to the music.

LOOK, EVERYONE!!

'Great!' says Jake. 'That's the principle locked down!'

Wow!! I can dance! I can't wait to add the music in and some leg moves too. OK . . . I can't dance, I can *only* arm dance. But how hard can *actual* dancing be? I'm already halfway there.

THE ALBERT HALL PRESENTS FOR ONE NIGHT ONLY . . . arm dance!

TICKETS IN HIGH DEMAND

SOLD OUT

I reckon I'd be quite happy to do our dance routine on stage at the science show now and I

guess it just *might* be more
attention-grabbing than
actual science!

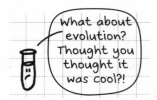

We walk all the way home arm dancing in time
with each other and Jake says
that we can do a proper rehearsal
later that evening with legs and
everything!

He suggests we go get changed
into something more 'dancey'
and meet in half an hour.

'Mum will be pleased if I'm out of the house,'
he says. 'Then she can be on the phone for hours
having secret conversations or
doing her online gambling or
whatever it is she needs me out
of the way for!'

'What about your brothers and sister?' I ask.

'They're not suspicious like me. She doesn't mind
having *them* around.
They're too young to
be bothered about what
she's up to. I hope it's
nothing illegal.'

When I get home, there's a huge bouquet of flowers in the hallway. Nani points at it, grinning, and passes me the card that came with them before heading back into the living room to watch TV. The envelope reads 'Flowers especially for you' in swirly writing. Especially for who? Me? I doubt it. Who would give *me* flowers?

Most likely they're a 'Get Well Soon' present for Nahid. But she isn't even here and they'd be dead by the time she next comes home, so I may as well open the card. Besides, they aren't even addressed to her. I steam the envelope open using the kettle like I've seen on telly. I'm really careful so that I don't burn myself.

CAUTION: HOT

Inside the envelope is a card with a big red heart on it. OMG!!!! Nahid has a secret admirer! I open the card and read the message.

Valerie,
I know we are meant to be a secret, but every time I think of you I want to send you flowers. I feel like I have won the lottery.
WINNER WINNER CHICKEN DINNER!!
M.H. xx

There's only one Valerie round here . . . and that's Jake's mum! That's it! Jake's mum has a fancy man! One with the initials M.H. who likes chicken dinners! Or perhaps it's a coded message . . .

Now, how does this code wheel work again?

Nani must have taken the flower delivery in as everyone was out next door. I quickly re-seal the envelope with a glue stick and race over to Jake's house. I put the flowers on the doorstep in the hope that Jake's mum gets to them before Jake does. There's no way I want Jake to know about this . . . his mum has a secret admirer! Jake won't like this one little bit . . .

CHAPTER 8

Rehearsals

I change into my 'danciest' outfit: my bobbly jogging bottoms, a sequined sweatshirt that Nahid grew out of years ago and my trusty trainers. I top it all off with a purple headband to keep my hair out of my face.

Not bad! I look like I'm about to go to an aerobics class!

Left arm down . . . and right arm up!

I practise some arm moves in the mirror. Like it.

I head next door to get Jake and notice that the flowers are still on the doorstep. Uh-oh. I don't want Jake to see them so I quickly move them to the side of the driveway. This way, only Jake's mum will see

them when she gets in
or out of her car.

Jake answers the door clutching a portable speaker, and we head off to the green. There are still some senior kids milling about, but luckily no Vicky or DJ. Phew. Jake puts on some tracks and we do the arm moves. We're in time with both the music and each other . . . so far, so good! He then tries to add in some leg moves, but that doesn't go as smoothly . . .

Doing both at once is much trickier.

He then drops the bombshell that this is just two bars of eight counts and that we need to dance for about THIRTY bars of eight counts!

Adding in the leg moves seems to be one step too far for me. It's a bit like that thing where you try to pat your head and rub your tummy in a circle at the same time . . . tricky to coordinate!

It's like my mind can't focus on remembering all the moves. No matter how hard I try to concentrate, it wanders off and I start thinking about other stuff . . .

Jake is being really patient with me. You also have to remember to keep your head up, shoulders back and stomach in and to smile the whole time. SO unnatural! I feel contorted.

I keep forgetting to smile as I'm too busy trying to focus on counting out the numbers!! Safe to say, I'm pretty bad at this.

At that moment, DJ and Vicky turn up.

Noooooooooooooooooo!

'Jake, can we stop?' I plead.

'Don't be silly,' he replies. 'You'll get the hang of it. It just takes time.'

Such patience. I'm all arms and legs and I'm not *even* in time any more.

It looks fine, honest, just needs a bit of work . . .

'I really don't want Vicky and DJ to see it till I can actually *do* it,' I plead with Jake desperately.

'They're hanging out with their high-school gang across the way,' he says. 'They won't bother about what we're doing.' Jake is getting a bit exasperated with me now.

It looks fine, honest, just needs a bit of work . . .

I wouldn't want them to see you being this bad, anyway . . .

We try again and I flail about for a couple more bars before stopping for a glug of water from my drinking bottle, which luckily I had the foresight to bring with me.

Well done, Einstein!

Dancing is energetic work. Jake takes a swig from his own bottle and then . . .

'Heyyyyy!' calls out the familiar voice of Vicky Chen.  Oh no. I spin round. She and DJ are heading in our direction.

'Can we check out your dance sequence?' asks DJ.

'We can give you some pointers if you like?' adds Vicky.

This is horrific.

'Err . . . it's not ready yet!' I say quickly.

'Well, that's OK. Show us what you have so far,' replies Vicky. 'You'll have to perform it at rehearsals tomorrow anyway, so you may as well get some feedback from us now before you finish working on it.'

I feel sick. I can't bear for them to see my appalling dance moves. They'll just laugh at me and I'll never be able to show my face at school again.

'Go on!' says DJ, nudging Jake.

'Errr . . . OK, I guess,' he says. 'Let me cue up the music.'

Before Jake has a chance to cue up anything, I yelp, 'I need the loo and I can't hold it in. I'm going

home!' and then run off,
leaving the three of them
standing there totally bemused.

I leg it all the way home like a mad woman.
Was that a bit extreme? Why did I say I
needed the loo when I could have just
said I was late for dinner or something?

Why didn't Jake say we were saving our
performance for a surprise or that we weren't ready
to show it to them yet? He knew I didn't want to do
it in front of Vicky and DJ. Talk
about dropping me in it.

Some friend he is.

When I get home, Jake's mum's flowers are still in
the driveway. They haven't been
noticed yet and instead they've
been driven over, squashed flat.
Oh dear.

I pick up the mangled flowers and put them on
the doorstep. Hmm, I think. There I was looking
out for Jake and meanwhile he was prepared to
embarrass me in front of DJ and Vicky! It's not *my*
fault if Jake sees the flowers first. Although that will
really upset him . . . I know, I'll ring the doorbell,

then run home, and hopefully they'll get intercepted by his mum . . .

Jake's baby brother

At school the next morning, Keziah and I try to work out who the flowers could be from. Someone with the initials M.H. . . .

The top suspects:

1. Mr Hamza. He owns the grocery store around the corner, but I'm pretty sure his first name is Ali. Although the note did say 'Winner, winner, chicken dinner' and his shop definitely sells chicken. He's very jokey. Not sure he's Jake's mum's type.

    Mr Hamza

2. Dr Hammond. I can imagine Valerie with a doctor – she'd love that. Good, respectable, professional! Unsure of his first name though. He's our local GP, but he is very young and Mum said the other week that he'd just got engaged, so that makes him a pretty unlikely suspect.

    Dr Hammond

3. Mariusz. He's a handyman that my parents recommended to Jake's parents when they first moved in. He's done loads of jobs round Jake's house. He looks a bit like a film star and I've seen Jake's mum giggling with him before. They have a good rapport!

Mariusz

4. Marcus Hartnell – that's the name of a local estate-agent firm. I've seen the name on 'For Sale' signs, including the one on Jake's house before he moved in. Maybe Marcus Hartnell is the owner of the agency and is now dating Valerie?

Marcus Hartnell

5. Mr Hastings – our very own deputy head. Eugh! Imagine! Jake would not like that one little bit. Can't remember his first name, so not 100 per cent positive about this one either.

Mr Hastings

Keziah points out that 'chicken dinner' could be a reference to Nando's, which is where Axel spotted Mr Hastings with Miss Rai. Maybe he took Valerie there too!

I hope you like it

I bring all my dates here

We can't think of any other eligible men – or any men – with the initials M.H. Let's face it, it could easily be someone we're not even aware of from the book club or Jake's mum's work.

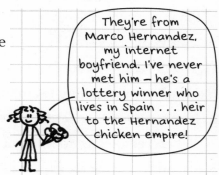

They're from Marco Hernandez, my internet boyfriend. I've never met him – he's a lottery winner who lives in Spain . . . heir to the Hernandez chicken empire!

There are so many possibilities.

I wonder whether Jake intercepted the flowers or whether his mum got to them first. I say flowers . . . they

R.I.P.

looked more like weeds after they'd been run over.

Fortunately, when he enters the classroom Jake seems pretty upbeat, so he definitely hasn't seen them. He heads over to me and Keziah.

'What's up?' he asks. We look shifty. 'Why are you guys being all secretive now? Seriously? You should hang out with my mum!'

Oh Valerie, you're such fun!

And we love your air of secrecy!

Why, thanks!!

He huffs off in a mood. I feel a bit bad, but I'm still not over the moon that he was prepared to throw me under the bus and get me to do my

rubbish dance moves in front of Vicky and DJ yesterday. Ugh! I'm really not looking forward to performing them in front of everyone later . . .

When rehearsals do finally come around, things are even worse than I expected because Hastings and Chen have come to watch. It's bad enough having to face Vicky and DJ after running away yesterday . . . but now this too? I feel ill. Maybe I could twist my ankle or something to get me out of performing . . .

Hooray, my foot's stuck in a bucket! I'll have to go to A&E

It doesn't help matters that Jake has got the hump with me! Dance partners require chemistry, according to *Strictly Come Dancing*, Jake's favourite Saturday-night telly show. No such luck here.

It's a unanimous zero from our judges for lack of chemistry!

I needn't worry, though, because I never get to bust out my moves. After watching the first three acts, Chen and Hastings are far from impressed.

'This science show lacks science! This isn't an episode of

Even the dancers lack chemistry

What's chemistry got to do with science?

Britain's Got Talent!' declares Hastings angrily.

Whoa! He wasn't even having an 'angry day' before now. He actually smiled on entering the room and told a sciencey joke . . .

Why are chemists good at problem solving? Because they have a lot of solutions!

Not bad for a 'teacher joke'.

'Vicky, this is not good enough!' says Mrs Chen to her daughter, who is squirming. 'I'm deeply disappointed. You should know better! A science show without science? Come on!'

Welcome to the animal show! We don't have animals but later I'll ride a tiny bicycle!!

'Maybe we should just call the whole thing off!' says Hastings. Vicky lets out an audible yelp.

'Martin, that might be a little hasty,' interjects Mrs Chen.

Hasty . . . that's what my last girlfriend nicknamed me. My, I'm glad we broke up!

'Fine!' he snaps. 'We'll give them a week to turn it around. Otherwise the show gets cancelled.'

And with that, the teachers leave.

Vicky Chen is quietly crying in the corner of the room and being comforted by her senior-school pals.

A week?! We'll need a small miracle to turn this all-singing, all-dancing extravaganza around into anything sciencey, especially with Vicky Chen at the helm. What on earth are we going to do?!

CHAPTER 9

The School Website

Vicky is sitting on a desk with her knees up and her head in her arms, whimpering inconsolably. I feel sorry for her. It's pretty embarrassing being told off, and *worse still* being told off in front of your friends, and *even worse still* being told off by your own mother, and *even worse than that* being told off by your own mother who also happens to be a teacher. Poor Vicky.

I'm also the Queen of England and I'll tell you off more in my next Queen's Speech!

Can't be fun crying uncontrollably in front of all of us either. And to think *I* felt embarrassed about running away from the green when I couldn't bear to show her and DJ our dance routine. I feel a lot better about that all of a sudden!

Nice to know I'm not the only one with misfortune!!

Mrs Chen really should have got the science club seniors to help organise the science show, not the drama club! I mean, she'd never get the science club to help put on the nativity . . .

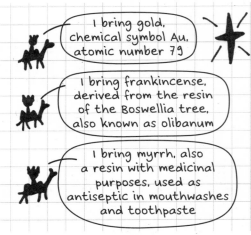

I bring gold, chemical symbol Au, atomic number 79

I bring frankincense, derived from the resin of the Boswellia tree, also known as olibanum

I bring myrrh, also a resin with medicinal purposes, used as antiseptic in mouthwashes and toothpaste

Keziah nudges me with excitement.

'Did you hear what I heard?' she asks with a glint in her eye.

'Errr . . . yeah,' I reply. 'The science show is about to get cancelled because it contains NO science! Something *I* pointed out a long time ago!'

What have you got?

SINCE!

'Not that!' she says. 'Chen called Hastings Martin! M.H.! Martin Hastings. *He* could be our man!'

104

'Oh yeah!' I say. 'Martin! That's right! I've heard him called that before. I remember now. Winner, winner, chicken dinner! We know he likes Nando's! It makes perfect sense! Jake will not be happy about this!'

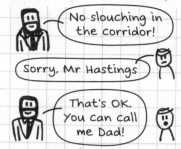

'Jake won't be happy about what?' asks Jake, appearing from out of nowhere.

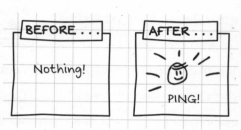

'We're gonna have to ditch our dance routine!' I say quickly. 'Either that or we'll have to add some science into it somehow!'

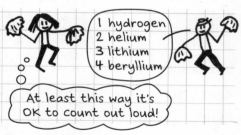

'That's it!' says Vicky, who's listening in nearby. She sits bolt upright as though someone has rebooted her.

'You and your friends are into science, Cookie! You can help us add some into each of the acts!'

'Great idea, Vick!' says DJ, high-fiving her. Suddenly all eyes are on me, Jake and Keziah.

Some of the eyes looking at us

'You can be our scientific advisory committee!' squeals Vicky as if she's never been upset at all. 'You can help advise everyone on how best to "science up" their acts. We'll start with Suzie and Alison's gymnastics display.'

'We're fine doing it ourselves, thanks,' protests Suzie.

We could wear 'I Love Science' tops!

No!

We could do it to sciencey music!

No!

'But we hate science,' says Alison.

We could have test tubes on our hair grips!

No!

'Oh yeah, good point,' says Suzie, caving in.

One by one, we slowly convert our primary-school version of *Britain's Got Talent* into a proper school science show. The senior kids listen to all our suggestions and chip in their own ideas too. This feels good.

My favourite conversions:

1. Magic show – now demonstrating and explaining magical chemical reactions.

   THEN → NOW

2. Gymnastics display – now a display with narration showing how gravity, balance, momentum and force work.

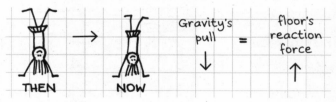

   THEN → NOW

   Gravity's pull ↓ = floor's reaction force ↑

3. Tayo's 'love of life' rap is now Tayo's 'love of science' rap.

   Livin' in da hood, feeling pretty good . . .

   It would be defiance to not believe in science . . .

It's a vast improvement! Plus, it's really fun working out how to convert all the acts to make them sciencey. Even better, Jake and I no longer have a dance sequence. HOOOOOOOOOORRR-RRAAAAYYYYYYY!!!!!!

Instead, we're now acting out a mini play, which is an ode to Ada Lovelace. Jake plays Charles Babbage and I'm Ada.

We add in lots of other sketches too – all odes to various scientists. Suzie Ashby plays Marie Curie, who discovered the elements of polonium and radium, which led to the invention of X-rays. Axel plays Albert Einstein, who came up with the theory of relativity. ↓

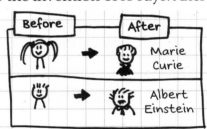

THEORY OF RELATIVITY = A very clever theory explaining how space, time and motion relate to each other.

The scientist sketches are dotted about in between all the other acts, so suddenly the whole thing feels a lot more sciencey. All the people who wanted small roles get to be narrators instead of just shaking pom-poms in the opening dance sequence.

I actually get lines. Amazing!

It seems sad to get rid of the whole opener, as it's really fun and the dance is pretty eye-catching, so we decide to keep it just to grab the audience's attention.

I actually get lines and to shake pom-poms. Wow!

We also add some of Jake's dance moves into the opening number since we're no longer doing our own dance. This keeps him and Vicky happy, not to mention Suzie and Alison, who can still cartwheel in!

HOORAY! We've managed to keep something irrelevant in!

We all leave rehearsals on a high. I'm in Vicky's and DJ's good books again, which is a huge relief after running away from them in such an absurd manner yesterday evening. Phew!

She's actually OK, that Cookie girl!

Yeah, even if she does have a weak bladder

When I get home, I'm dying to tell Nani all about saving the science show, but sadly she doesn't understand a word I'm saying. She's grinning away and nodding, but I know she's just humouring me. She has no idea what I'm going on about.

It's so frustrating. I can't even communicate with my own nani. I sigh, head to the kitchen and grab a bag of Bombay mix. I study the packet as I munch away. It has pictures of funny little Bombay mix characters on the back.

The characters all have their names written in Bengali with the English underneath.

I recognise lots of the letters from my name (and my sisters') and realise that it's not that hard to match up some of the letters and sounds.

I remember that *khushi* is the Bengali word for 'happy'. I know this because Roubi mentioned it when we first got the *Khushi's Quest* game. I work out how to write 'Cookie's happy' in Bengali, then show Nani, who is really impressed.

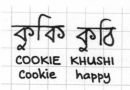

COOKIE KHUSHI
Cookie happy

She reads it out and I teach her the English translation: Cookie's happy. Yay! She understands what I mean! Then Nani writes something herself and says in English: 'Nani's happy!'

NANI KHUSHI

We chuckle and have a hug. I'm making progress at this language thing! Using some of the Bengali newspaper that was wrapping the veg Nani smuggled over and the Bombay mix packet (both of which have bits of English translation on), we have a great little communication session!

রিবস (cook rib)
কুক
I dunno how to say chicken!

We don't eat pork!

Nani is fun and cheeky. We have a proper laugh!

ha ha

hee hee

The next morning, I give Dad a note I've written in Bengali.

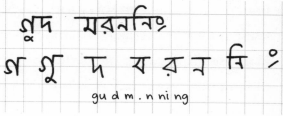

gu d m . n ni ng

'Gud moronin,'
he reads. 'Ah, I
see, you mean good morning! Hey, that's really
impressive!'

'Moron-ing? Makes no sense?' laughs Roubi.

I laugh as well. I can now write coded messages
to Dad! But the code is
Bengali!

If I teach Keziah and
Jake the basics then we can
pass notes to each other in
Bengali too. Awesome!

I pass Dad
another note . . .

'Gud bee,' he says, before correcting my note to
read 'Goodbye'. Nani comes in.
'Goodbye!' She chuckles.

'See! Nani understands me!' I say as I leave the
house.

I see Valerie's squashed
bouquet looking a bit sorry for
itself as I walk past Jake's. It's now
in a vase displayed in the middle
of their downstairs bay window.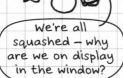

Maybe it's a coded message from Valerie to M.H. to let him know she's thinking of him.

At morning break, Keziah and I run to the library to do some more detective work on the computer. Hamza's grocery doesn't have a website, but we look up the local GP surgery and find out that Dr Hammond's first name is Luke. We eliminate him from our investigation.

We're about to see if Valerie is on Facebook when there's a commotion two computers along where Tina Mories is sitting. There's lots of whispering and sniggering. People begin to huddle around her screen.

Keziah and I wander over to see what's going on. Everyone is looking at the school website. The 'Meet the Teachers' page is up on the screen. I immediately notice the picture of Mr Hastings, labelled Martin Hastings.

'Well, *we* knew that was his name already!' I say.

'That's not what everyone's looking at!' replies Keziah. 'Look at Mrs Chen's entry!'

I read it . . .

Jocelyn Chen is Woodburn Primary's Science Lead, with a passion for STEM learning (Science, Technology, Engineering and Maths). She has been with the school for five years.

In an unmatching font, the website then goes on to say:

Little does everyone realise, she actually originally failed her chemistry GCSE! Not so clever now, huh, Mrs Chen?! Some science teacher you are!

The school staff have definitely not written this, nor have they even noticed it's been put up there. The school website has obviously been HACKED! But by who – and why?!

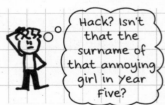

CHAPTER 10

Who's the Hacker?

Hmmmm. This is definitely the work of a disgruntled student. It's more likely to be someone

from Year Five or Six, as I reckon anyone younger wouldn't know how to hack.

> Hack? Isn't that the surname of that annoying girl in Year Five?

To be fair, most Year Fives and Sixes probably can't hack either. Because our topic at the moment is coding and computing, we've all got into code-breaking and puzzle-solving recently.

> Hope you're not passing notes

> No, just doing sudoku

> Er, I guess that's OK then!

We've even been discussing hacking in our

computer class with Mrs Chen. It could easily have put the idea into one of our classmates' heads . . .

Why am I wasting my time on sudoku when I could be doing cyber espionage?

There are a few suspects who I think would have a motive. The main motive being a dislike of Mrs Chen.

People who dislike Mrs Chen:

1. Suzie Ashby and Alison Denbigh – Mrs Chen once sent them to the green seats outside the head's office, as they were painting rainbows on their nails in class. They haven't liked her since.

    Mrs Chen is, like, sooooo uncool

2. Saul Roben – Saul is a climate-change denier! I know!!! It's a scientific fact that the earth is under threat from global warming, but this doesn't stop Saul trying to answer back to Mrs Chen. I think his dad has brainwashed him or something.

    Chen is a conspiracy theorist

3. Emma Matthewson – Emma believes in creationism and that Adam and Eve are the parents of all human beings and that we didn't evolve from apes. Mrs Chen certainly does not agree and makes no attempt to hide it!!

> Chen is a non-believer

4. Jake Kay – Jake also got 'green-seated' by Mrs Chen (along with me!!!). On top of that, he definitely knew that Mrs Chen failed her chemistry GCSE because *I* told him. That makes him the prime suspect right now, with both insider knowledge *and* a motive.

> Seriously, Cookie? Give me a break!

As far as I know, Jake, Keziah and I are the only ones who know about Mrs Chen failing chemistry . . . unless Jake or Keziah told someone else?

> Meanwhile, in the school playground . . .
>
> EVERYONE, CHEN FAILED CHEMISTRY!

Keziah didn't even tell *me* when Axel told her about seeing Hastings and Rai together in Nando's. She definitely isn't the weak link here. It has to be Jake.

> Seriously, Cookie? Give me a break!

Keziah and I decide to confront him . . .

'You have as much motive as I do!!' he protests. 'Chen smiled at you, giving you false hope, before announcing the science competition winners at the beginning of term. You totally turned against her then, remember? Plus, she "green-seated" you too!' He's hissing with rage.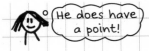

'He does have a point,' says Keziah.

I think about it . . .

I actually agree with him.

On the face of it, I have as much of a motive as he does. As well as that, the way he reacted has convinced that me he's innocent.

Back to the drawing board . . .

Maybe someone decoded our note after Mrs Mannan threw it in the bin?

I need some new leads.

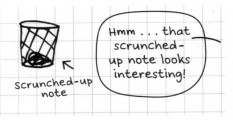

During science class, Mrs Chen is flustered and embarrassed. There's lots of sniggering and whispering. This must be so humiliating for her. She's even meeker and milder than usual, and we can barely hear anything she says now.

She won't even make eye contact with anyone. I really want to find the culprit. I feel kind of sorry for her.

At lunchtime, rumours are flying around that Hastings is cancelling the science show until someone owns up to the website hack. Noooooooooooooooooooo!! After all our hard work to turn it around! This is so unfair. I HAVE TO FIND THE CULPRIT!

Maybe Hastings hacked the website himself so that he could cancel the show once and for all? He's always been against it. He *definitely* knew about Chen failing chemistry, and it's very suspicious that nothing about *him* has been changed.

Vicky and DJ will be devastated about the show.

I notice that Tayo is showing Tina something in a computer magazine in the lunch queue and it dawns on me that we have two more suspects on our hands. Tayo is really into gaming and computers, and Tina is a dab hand at tech. Both might be capable of hacking . . .

Yes – they're both high scorers on Pac-Man!

Can't think what Tina's motive might be, but Tayo has always been a bit of a rebel. Hacking the school website is exactly the sort of thing he'd do . . .

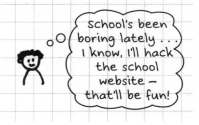

School's been boring lately . . . I know, I'll hack the school website – that'll be fun!

He probably didn't even think of the consequences and that it would end up upsetting his own brother. He couldn't have known the show would get cancelled as a result. If Vicky already knew that her mum failed chemistry, she could have easily told DJ, who could have easily told Tayo.

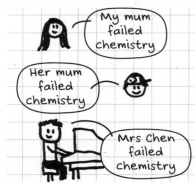

My mum failed chemistry

Her mum failed chemistry

Mrs Chen failed chemistry

I march over to see if I can get a confession out of him.

'Poor DJ!' I say, pulling Tayo aside. 'I just wanted you to know that *I* know, but I'm not gonna tell anyone. Yet . . .'

Tayo looks confused. 'Poor DJ?' he repeats.

'The school will know,' I declare. 'The system will show it.'

If Tayo's worried that there's a cyber trail that points to him, I reckon he might come clean. He pauses and then looks as though the penny has dropped . . .

'The school does know,' he says.

What?!! Now *I'm* confused.

'But he even uses DJ on exercise books. He's only Dorcan on exam papers.'

'Dorcan?' I say, baffled.

'Dorcan Julius . . . DJ!' says Tayo.

I know your secret

Just don't call me dork!

Dorc! It's spelled with a c!

Oh yeah!

'My mum was convinced he was gonna be a girl,' he continues. 'She wanted to name him Dorcas after someone in the Bible. When she had a boy, she switched it to Dorcan. That is what you meant, right?' he asks.

'Errrr, yeah . . . Dorcan,' I mumble.

Great! Now I know another person's secret! Tayo clearly has no idea about the hacking. Double great. Dorcan Julius?!! Didn't see that coming!!

When we get home, there's a car parked in Jake's drive that's definitely not his mum's.

'Oh no, whose car is that?' he says. 'Will you come in? I'm not in the mood to entertain guests. We can go in and run straight up to my room and say we've got homework to do.'

We go in and run straight up to Jake's room and say we've got homework to do. Jake's mum is laughing with a man in the kitchen.

I look out of Jake's window and notice that the car in the drive has a bumper sticker on it.

NO TOOLS ARE LEFT OVERNIGHT IN THIS CAR

I note down the number plate to see if it matches the one I took down the other night when his mum came back late from 'book club'.

'I wonder who your mum's guest is,' I say nosily.

'Dunno.' Jake shrugs. 'But thank goodness she didn't call us in to find out!'

Amazingly, we actually do end up finishing our homework, but it's much more fun doing it together than doing it solo. When it's time to leave, I pop into the kitchen to say goodbye to Jake's mum and she appears from under the kitchen counter, as does the man!!

'Just looking at a leak under the kitchen sink!' she says, a little flustered.

'Uh, OK,' I reply. 'Just saying hi and bye! Errr . . . by the way, what are you reading at book club at the moment?'

'*How to Fix your Plumbing!* by Lee Keytap.' The man laughs. Valerie chuckles too. I don't. Interesting that she doesn't actually say what she *is* reading.

That's if she is actually reading anything at all.

Book club?! It's not an actual book club, it's just the name of the pub I go to!

Will, Jake's little brother, enters the kitchen and starts giving a running commentary on what's going on, as per usual.

'Hello, Mariusz Kowalski. I see you're under the sink with my mother. Hello, Cookie Haque. Didn't know you were here. Just taking biscuits to Helen, as, being a big sister, she's bossed me to do so,' he says, exiting the room as quickly as he entered and grabbing an almost-finished pack of biscuits as he goes.

Before I leave, Mariusz gives me his card in case my parents need any more work done around the house.

No job too small!
* MARIUSZ HANDYMAN
* m.kowalski@mail.com
* 0789813251

At home, I try to see if the car number plates match up . . .

PO23 YIB

They do!! But Mariusz's initials are M.K. – Mariusz Kowalski – so that's no good. Could a K look like an H written down?

К П Н Н
Н К К Н

Nah . . .

Neither of my private investigations are going very well at the moment. They're both lacking any conclusive evidence. Sadly, M.H. and the hacker are both still at large and able to carry on their dealings undetected.

The next morning, as soon as I get into class Keziah bounds over to me and Jake.

'I've got it – I know who the hacker is!' she says. 'Axel saw the note too! He was next to me at the time and we both laughed at it.'

'He hates Chen,' I agree, nodding. 'She always gives him low marks. He has a motive and the means. It could totally be Axel!'

I could imagine Axel being an excellent hacker. We all look over at him. He's in his seat twisting a rubber band round the end of his finger so it's all red and bulbous.

But before we can approach him, Tina Mories enters the classroom excitedly and loudly declares, 'THERE'S BEEN ANOTHER HACK!!'

CHAPTER 11

Rumours

The hacker has struck again! This time Mr Hastings' teacher profile has been changed. It reads . . .

Martin Hastings has been with Woodburn Primary School for over eight years. Under his deputy headship the school has leapt from Good to Outstanding Ofsted status.

But then, in an unmatching font, it goes on to say:

Quite surprising, considering he couldn't even pass his driving test! Having failed it SEVEN times, it would be fair to say perhaps he is going for a Guinness World Record! What a LOSER!

This latest revelation convinces me that Hastings is definitely NOT the hacker. But, more importantly, it reminds me that he can't even drive! I'd forgotten that. He couldn't possibly have dropped Valerie home the other night.

> Thought you were driving me home

> I was, but I can't drive

So, Martin Hastings is NOT the hacker or M.H. Dropped from both investigations in one fell swoop.

> Charming!

> But you're innocent!

> Oh yeah – hooray!

This does not bode well for the science show – Hastings will be on the war path now. If the cancellation rumours are true, no amount of additional science will save it.

> We've turned the show into a two-hour lecture on how great science is!

> Still not sciencey enough!

> But sir . . .

> No buts! CANCELLED!

Meanwhile, Keziah confronts Axel about whether or not he's the hacker. He denies it, but he's blatantly the only other person who knew everything. Keziah believes him. I'm in two minds so I'm gonna keep a close eye on him.

> Back off, Cookie . . . it's a bit much!

At break time, we all hang out together and Axel tells us that he's learnt how to write in invisible ink from a book he has at home.

Invisible ink is basically just diluted lemon juice.

If you dip a fountain pen or cotton bud in it, then use it to write on paper, the writing disappears when it dries and then reappears again when you put it on a heater. I have to say, it's pretty cool.

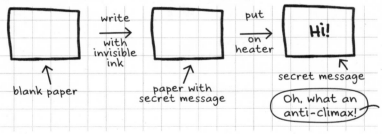

I make a mental note to try it out later to see if it actually works. But right now, I'm not going to let this distract me. I'm still watching you, Axel Kahn, number-one hacking suspect.

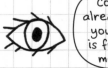

At lunchtime he's acting a bit shifty. I wonder if I can catch him in the act. He slips out of the dinner hall really quickly, leaving half of his fish and chips uneaten.

Bizarre behaviour. And stranger still to totally skip dessert. Extremely odd indeed. I slip out after him, keeping a good distance between us.

He's clutching a piece of paper and ducks into the school library. I knew it! The paper probably has the next hack on it. He must be going in there to type it up on a computer. Should I hang back or catch him in the act? After some deliberation, I decide to go in, but it's too late – he is already coming back out empty-handed!

BINGO! The paper with the evidence on it will still be in the library! I've got him. I go in and rifle through the wastepaper baskets . . . no paper in any of them!

It's not on any of the tables either. How odd. I scan the room and notice three sheets of paper on a radiator round the back of a reference bookshelf.

The papers appear to be blank, but then I look more closely and see that Axel has been testing out invisible ink on them. As if by magic, while I'm looking at the paper, writing appears . . .

The writing has turned light brown while resting on the heater. Amazing!! I quickly look up an explanation of the science behind it in a library book . . . may as well while I'm here!

The invisible-ink trick is a pretty clever one, it has to be said. Axel has clearly been using the lemon slice from his fish and chips (!!!), as I can see it in one of the bins.

The fact that I've not caught him red-handed doesn't rule Axel out of my hacking

investigation. It just shows me quite how much he's into secrecy and message writing, so he's still very much a suspect . . . perhaps even more so than before!

When I get home later that day, Nani is watching *Mr Bean* on the telly and chuckling away. I join her on the sofa and we feast on the Bombay mix crisp things together, exchanging little bits and pieces of Bengali and English that we've taught one another.

Nani loves *Mr Bean*. She watches it back in Bangladesh too. I didn't even realise it was on over there! I'm having so much fun hanging out with her these days. She's a real laugh and loves joking about. It's amazing how much we can actually communicate with the

odd word, facial expressions and lots of pointing.

After *Mr. Bean* has finished, she goes upstairs to pray. She does it five times a day – now that's dedication!!

Praying is my mindfulness

Mum says there's not much else to do in the village anyway so she may as well pray!

I pray that if I pray lots, in the afterlife I won't live in a village with nothing to do but pray all day!

Just as well she doesn't have Skype . . . She and

Wish I had Skype! Oh well, I'll just pray instead of Skyping

I pray I get Skype!

Mum would be gassing all day long!

She taught me some of her prayer moves. They're much easier to remember than Jake's dance moves!!

She also taught me that you have to face east from the UK while you're doing it because that's where the holy city of Mecca is.

Plus, you have to wash your hands and mouth first.

While Nani's upstairs praying, I decide to play some computer games. It's been a while since I played *Khushi's Quest*. Huh?!! There's ANOTHER new high score that isn't mine!

KHUSHI'S QUEST

NEW HIGH SCORE
ILC 730721

That's so strange. I thought the last mystery score was from Nahid playing it when she was sofa-bound. But she's not around any more so it can't be her. Very weird. This time it's not even under my user profile but a new one: ILC. Maybe it's Roubi? Perhaps ILC stands for International Labour Convention or something else political-sounding? I didn't realise she was so good at gaming.

POLITICS

This afternoon, Mum gets back from her away-break to Nahid's uni flat. She says Nahid's getting really muscly from walking around on crutches

133

the whole time. Ha! No one to boss about at uni demanding your slippers be fetched from upstairs!!

Can you get my slippers from upstairs?

We live in a flat

Oh yeah!

At least she's getting some exercise and not just sitting on the sofa all day hogging the cushions.

Who needs dumbbells when you have crutches!

A flyer comes through our letterbox asking if we want to have our house valued. Mum says that the house opposite ours has just gone up for sale. She saw a board being put up last week and bumped into the estate agent, Mr Hartnell, who was chatting to Valerie from next door. He'd been doing a valuation on the house.

Cookie Haque lives opposite? Hmm . . . that'll put the value of your house down!

Mr Hartnell, hey? Chatting to Valerie, hey? So . . . Marcus Hartnell is a real person? A person who knows Valerie! Exciting times! A major suspect for the M.H. mystery, especially as that was the estate agent that Jake's house was bought through.

I know, if I sell her a house then maybe she'll like me and I can move into it!

It's good to finally be making some progress. Wish I could work out how to find out for sure if Axel is the hacker or not. Keziah reckons that if it was him, he'd have written about Miss Rai being in Nando's with Hastings in her teacher profile. Maybe that's coming next? Talking of which, that secret wasn't very well kept after all. Roubi told me that she heard from someone in Year Eight that Miss Rai got engaged to her fiancé Fernando in the summer holidays!!!!

> There's something hard and crunchy on my peri-peri wrap!

> It's a ring! Will you marry me?

Engaged, indeed!!! I reckon this is a classic case of misinformation where each time the message gets changed a bit through word of mouth until it doesn't resemble the truth at all.

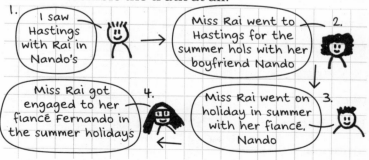

1. I saw Hastings with Rai in Nando's

2. Miss Rai went to Hastings for the summer hols with her boyfriend Nando

3. Miss Rai went on holiday in summer with her fiancé, Nando

4. Miss Rai got engaged to her fiancé Fernando in the summer holidays

It does gives me a great idea, though. Now I know exactly how I can find out if Axel is our hacker.

CHAPTER 12

The Trap!

The next day I tell Keziah and Jake that what we need is our very own rumour. We have to make up something totally convincing about one of the teachers and tell Axel in confidence. If it then appears on the school website, we'll know that Axel is the hacker. It's a foolproof plan.

Yes, it was me all along, and I would have gotten away with it if it wasn't for you pesky kids!

We all look over at him. He seems so innocent, fiddling with his rubber

If I make these silly messages and keep winding rubber bands around my finger, it will throw them off the scent of my world-class computer espionage

bands and writing funny invisible-ink messages.

The thing is, there's really no one else apart from Axel who it *could* be. At least setting this 'trap' will let us know one way or the other. We decide to make something up about Mr Edwards, the PE teacher.

'We could say that before he was a PE teacher he was a real wimp and couldn't even do one press-up,' pipes up Jake. 'And now he can do them with just one arm!'

'Or how about that his hair fell out after he got hit on the head by a cricket ball?' I suggest.

'Can that happen?' asks Keziah

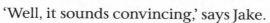

'I think so,' I reply.

'Well, it sounds convincing,' says Jake.

Mr Edwards is almost completely bald. He often wears a cap and has recently started growing a stubbly beard. It looks good on him.

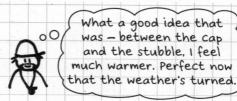

We decide to let Axel overhear the 'fake news' at some point during lunch break. After we've eaten,

instead of going out to play, we all have to attend an emergency meeting that's been scheduled by Vicky and DJ to try to rescue the science show.

Emergency!!

What? Has the Prime Minister resigned?

No, the science show may or may not be cancelled!

Vicky and DJ seem to have become quite fond of our science-show group now. At first, I thought

they wouldn't be that into it, but it feels good to know they're really rooting for us.

We did say we LOVE science!

Well at least they're not spelling it SINCE now I guess

Axel is nowhere to be seen at lunch. Maybe he's writing more invisible-ink messages in the library?

INVISIBLE-INK MESSAGES ARE BETTER THAN LUNCH!

MILK WORKS JUST AS WELL AS LEMON JUICE

I LOVE RUBBER BANDS!

Luckily, he pitches up to the emergency meeting. The atmosphere in the room is totally different to our regular rehearsals. Everybody seems mega serious and intense. Even Suzie and Alison have stopped clowning around. Vicky clears her throat and walks to the front of the hubbub.

'We have a crisis situation,' she declares. 'All our hard work is in jeopardy. We need the teachers to understand that we shouldn't be penalised for the actions of others. It's totally unfair.'

Wow! Vicky is rousing the crowd and showing real leadership potential here. She's so confident and stateswoman-like. It's as though she's a politician or something. I can see why she's so good at drama.

'I want you all to get together in groups of four,' she continues. 'Each group needs to come up with a solution or strategy to help save the show.'

Keziah, Jake, Axel and I team up and start discussing ideas. We're sitting next to Tina Mories, Clare Kelly and the rest of their group, who are jotting down a load of bullet points. Typical, we're already behind. But then I notice Suzie Ashby and Alison Denbigh on the other side of us, plaiting each other's hair, much to the annoyance of the rest of their group, who are having to do all the legwork.

Now is the perfect opportunity to drop the fake Edwards rumour into the conversation.

'Hey! Get this, guys,' I say. 'I heard that Mr Edwards used to have thick, curly orange hair, but it fell out after he got hit on the head by a cricket ball!!'

Jake and Keziah laugh.
Axel looks pretty unfussed. Hmm.

'Sorry to interrupt your engrossing gossip session,' interjects Vicky. 'As fascinating as it is, can you all focus, please? We've got a show to save!'

'Uh, yeah, sorry, Vicky,' says Keziah.

'No biggie. It's just I know you guys can come up with something good!' She winks then walks off.

Axel smiles and tries to wink back, but it's kind of weird.

'Great goss, Cookie!' chimes in Jake. 'I'd heard that too. A cricket ball! Poor Edwards! Crazy, huh, Axel?'

'Errr . . . sure,' he replies. Axel seems totally uninterested. I'm not even convinced he's actually listening!

After ten minutes or so, Vicky asks for our suggestions, group by group. We all present our ideas. Suzie's group suggests a protest march.

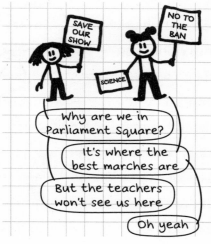

Another group says we should all go on strike . . .

And the group before ours says the show should
go ahead anyway
without school
backing. Now
that would be
interesting . . .

Our group is up next. We suggest going straight
to the top . . .

'The buck doesn't stop with Mr Hastings!' says

Jake. 'Sometimes
if you wanna get
things done, you
gotta go to the head
honcho.'

'Yeah!' chimes in
Keziah. 'We need to get
to Mrs De Souza. She's
above Mr Hastings. She
can overrule him.'

DJ is nodding away.
It looks like he and
Vicky like this idea.

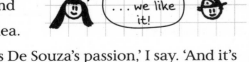

'Science is Mrs De Souza's passion,' I say. 'And it's
a major focus of our school. It would be madness to

cancel the show. I know
she'll see sense if we just
reason with her.'

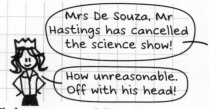

'You guys are right!' Vicky says, nodding in agreement. 'Woodburn prides itself on its science record. I reckon this plan might just work. Cookie, you're outspoken and into science. Can we trust *you* with this?'

Huh?

'OK,' I reply, half flattered and half dreading it.

'Great!' replies Vicky. 'So, gang, let's reconvene in a few days. That should give Cookie and her group enough time to get cracking with their mission! Here's my number if you need to get in touch.'

Vicky hands me
a business card with
all her details on it.
Vicky Chen has a
business card!!!

Suzie looks jealous that I've been
given a direct line to Vicky. Oh help!
I'd better deliver now. The pressure!

I'm not at all sure that
I can convince Mrs
De Souza to reinstate
the science show.

The AUDACITY! Thinking she could sweet-talk me and undermine Mr Hastings. OFF WITH HER HEAD!

I need to find that hacker, and fast! That would
be a sure-fire way to get the show back on the road.
I only have a few days for Axel to do the next hack
about Edwards's bald head . . .
if indeed Axel is the hacker.

I'm not

If I catch him then the
science show will be reinstated. But if he's innocent,
shouldn't we all
go and convince
De Souza to
reinstate the
show? Why
should I be the
one to do it?!
The whole group
would have to

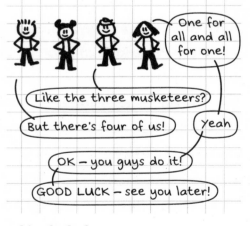

One for all and all for one!

Like the three musketeers?

But there's four of us!

Yeah

OK – you guys do it!

GOOD LUCK – see you later!

come with me – Axel included.

On the way home from school, I notice the
Marcus Hartnell 'For Sale' board on the house
opposite and make a mental note to mention him

in front of Valerie when I next see her. Her reaction should tell me if he's M.H.

It seems both investigations are coming along nicely now. And, as if on cue, when I get home Keziah calls . . .

'Get on your computer now!!' she cries. 'It's just gone up on the school website.'

I log on and take a look. Lo and behold, Mr Edwards's description on the 'Meet the Teachers' page reads:

In the three years that Hamish Edwards has been with Woodburn Primary, his enthusiasm for physical education has been infectious, extending even to other members of teaching staff, who he managed to train up to compete in the Ealing Half Marathon this year, raising a fantastic £576.28 for the PTA.

Then, in a different font, the website goes on to say:

His enthusiasm is not matched in amount by his hair, however, which fell out when he got hit on the head by a cricket ball. His brain function seems to have remained intact. We think . . .

OMG. That was quick. BINGO!!! Axel Kahn, you dark horse! You were taking it in all along, huh? Clever. You certainly had *me* fooled.

'That's great, Keziah!' I say. 'We've got him! The show is saved. Axel Kahn is the Woodburn Hacker!'

CHAPTER 13

Suspect at Large

The Woodburn Hacker. It makes him sound kind of vicious. This phone call has certainly taken a turn for the worse.

DAILY NEWS
Suspect at large
Schoolboy Axel Kahn is the Woodburn Hacker *contd*

Oh, Axel! What have you done? I really didn't want it to be Axel. Keziah feels the same.

'I just don't believe it!' she says. 'He's so harmless and sweet.'

Butter wouldn't melt in my mouth!

'I know,' I agree. 'But some of the best criminals are good at putting up a front.'

I'm just a hairdresser, honest. Here, have a pie!

Sweeney Todd, the demon barber of Fleet Street

'It makes no sense,' says Keziah. 'I mean, what would his motive be?

I know he doesn't like Mrs Chen, but he has nothing against any of the other teachers. To be totally honest, I don't even think he cares enough to be mean about teachers on the school website.'

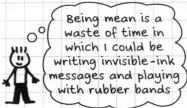

Being mean is a waste of time in which I could be writing invisible-ink messages and playing with rubber bands

'Well, I guess maybe he dislikes Mr Hastings cos he was trying to cancel the science show?' I reply, not even managing to convince myself. 'And maybe Mr Edwards because Axel's not exactly the biggest fan of PE?'

VICTIM LIST
1. Chen
2. Hastings
3. Edwards

If I write this in invisible ink, no one will know but me!

I was stabbing in the dark here. I really didn't have a clue.

Where's my knife? Can't see . . .

'Besides,' I continue, 'criminals often get addicted to the buzz and the thrill of getting away with it. He was probably only intending to do Mrs Chen over, and then when he saw how easy it was he thought, why stop there?'

Mwah ha ha, this crime thing's a piece of cake. I will not stop until the whole school website is just a bunch of rubbish!

'But Axel's not even fussed about the science show,' Keziah protests. 'He wouldn't care if Hastings cancelled it!'

'Believe me, I'm just as disappointed as you,' I say.

'Well, I'm not actually disappointed at all cos I don't think it's true!' says Keziah, raising her voice a little. Odd. So unlike her to get riled.

'You're very defensive of Axel,' I say, also raising my voice. 'I hope you'd be this protective over me if *I* got involved in criminal activity!'

Yuck! I'm sounding jealous.

'Look, I gotta go,' she replies, 'my dad's calling me for dinner.'

Great. I think Keziah's annoyed with me, all because of my relentless pursuit of justice. I decide to call Jake to gauge his thoughts . . .

'Hello!' A man's voice I vaguely recognise answers the phone.

'Errrr, is Jake there?' I say.

'Hang on . . .' replies the voice. There's a pause. 'Val! It's for Jake!'

There are some muffled noises. Why is a man answering Jake's landline? Could that be M.H.? After a few seconds, Jake's brother Will picks up . . .

Oh brother!!

'Hello! Jake is in the bath. I prefer showers to baths. Showers are more environmentally friendly. They use less water. I could use a drink of water. Did you know the chemical formula of water is H_2O because a water molecule has two atoms of hydrogen bonded to one atom of oxygen? Oxygen is the name of the nightclub where Mummy and Daddy met . . .'

'Will!' I interrupt. 'Who answered the phone?'

'Mariusz Kowalski. But Mummy calls him Mariusz Handyman. That's what it says in her phone. She often can't remember stuff, so she puts people's names in wrong. She put your mum's name in as Rozie Next Door and she put the babysitter's name in as Rachel Babysitter, even though those aren't their surnames . . .'

Blah blah blah . . .

'Will, I gotta go! Get Jake to call me. Bye!' I hang up.

M.H.! Mariusz Handyman! Of course!! And his number plate matched with the car from the night Valerie was dropped home from her supposed 'book club'. This is exciting! Both investigations are making proper progress now!

Mariusz Handyman

Marcus Hartnell

I look through my schoolbag for the piece of paper on which I scrawled down Mariusz's number plate when I was at Jake's the other day. I find the business card he gave me, which says 'Mariusz Handyman' on it in big lettering.

No job too small!
* MARIUSZ HANDYMAN
* m.kowalski@mail.com
* 0789813251

I study the card closely to see if there are any more clues on it. I'm not sure what I'm looking for – it's not as though he'd put a picture of a chicken dinner on there! I use this as an opportunity to clear out my bag, which is full of crumbs and miscellaneous debris, including the Science Museum leaflet for the computing exhibition that Mrs Chen gave us.

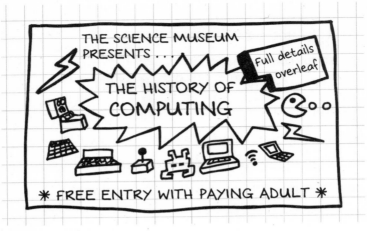

Now *this* I wanna go to. I run downstairs and stick the leaflet on the fridge with a magnet that says 'Important' on it.

This way I won't lose it. Things always seem to get lost in my schoolbag. The phone rings – it's Jake.

'How come the handyman is answering your landline now?' I ask. '*He's* making himself at home . . .'

Can I have another tea, please?

'He was taking a look at the phone when you rang,' replies Jake. 'He'd come back to pick up a spanner he'd left here the other day, so Mum asked him to check the phone. It only rings on silent mode, so we never know when people have called.

We keep finding
messages on our
answerphone that
we had no idea
about!'

Totally plausible explanation, but also a good
cover story for Valerie in case Jake asks why
Mariusz is over again.
Hmmm. I fill Jake in on the
latest developments of my
hacker investigation.

He goes onto the school website to take a look.
Although he's initially sceptical about Axel's
involvement, he eventually
agrees it must be Axel – he
can't think of any other
explanation.

'Unless it's *you* doing it and you're trying to
frame Axel cos you're jealous that Keziah sits next
to him!' he teases.

Well, I hope he's
teasing me and not
outright accusing
me!

'Don't be ridiculous!' I protest. 'Why would I do *that* and jeopardise the science show?!'

'OMG!!!' he says excitedly. 'It's definitely not you! Come to the side window! Now!'

Huh?! I race to the window facing Jake's house and look out to see him waving his iPad at me. 'What?!' I say, confused.

My window   Jake's window

'Just now,' he replies, 'as we were speaking, I was on the school website and it changed right in front of me. Whoever the hacker is – they're hacking it right now! Look!!!'

I screw up my eyes. I can't possibly read the website off his iPad when I'm one whole house away. But then I spot it . . . the school logo has changed from an ink quill to a banana!!

As he's holding up the tablet, the webpage refreshes right before us and the words 'Woodburn Primary' change to 'Banana Primary'!

I'm running out of gossip – I'll randomly just change stuff to fruit, I guess!

Well, one thing's for sure – Jake definitely knows that I'm not the hacker!

What should we do about Axel? Should we confront him? Tell on him? Help him cover it up and get away with it? And what about the science show? Axel's our friend. I feel so confused about the whole thing.

'I know!' says Jake. 'Shall I call Axel right now and mention bananas? He'll squirm if I catch him red-handed! He'll probably confess everything to me!'

'Good idea!' I say. 'Ring me back straight back! I wanna know everything!'

While I'm waiting, I log on to our computer to take a look at the school website for myself.

But I don't have to wait long. Jake calls me back after a couple of minutes.

'So?' I ask. 'What happened?! Did he confess? Did he cry? Was he embarrassed? He didn't hang up on you, did he?'

'He wasn't in,' Jake replies.

'Oh,' I say.

I race downstairs to our home computer. It's still on the 'Meet the Teachers' page. Just then, the screen flickers and I notice that Miss Rai's teacher description has now changed so it reads:

A newcomer to Woodburn Primary, Jas Rai fitted in straight away as lead Reception teacher, ensuring children make a smooth transition from the free play of nursery years to the structured learning of the school classroom.

Then, in an unmatching font, the website goes on to say:

We wish her all the best in her recent marriage over the summer to deputy head Mr Hastings. The celebration was catered for by Nando's with a giant chicken-flavoured wedding cake!

MEANWHILE IN THE RUMOUR MILL . . .

NO WAY!! This *can't* be the work of Axel! This was the rumour mill in overdrive! Axel knows the *original* secret!

Mr Hastings and Miss Rai went to Nando's, but that was *all* that happened. Miss Rai didn't get engaged

like Roubi had heard, and as for getting married to Mr Hastings, that's total nonsense.

This new turn of events means that Axel is innocent and we're back to square one. The Woodburn Hacker is still at large and we have NO LEADS!

CHAPTER 14

Two Steps Forward, One Step Back

Axel definitely *isn't* the hacker. He was at the Science Museum with his mum when the hacks took place. She'd found the voucher for the computing exhibition in his schoolbag and decided to take him there.

He says there's a massive area in the basement with shedloads of computer games from over the years. There are really old-fashioned, low-tech ones with 8-bit graphics all the way through to swanky virtual-reality ones where you put on a headset and feel like everything is in 3D. Apparently, it's like being in the future.

Who you calling low-tech?

Axel's mum let them eat dinner in the museum restaurant and they stayed till the whole place closed, which is well past Axel's bedtime.

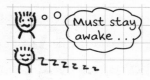
Must stay awake . .

Zzzzzz

He keeps yawning today!

He says that I have to go check it out and that I'd

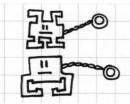

love it cos I love gaming. He even bought me and Keziah a Space Invader keyring each from the gift shop.

Axel is so sweet. I feel really bad for ever suspecting he might be the hacker. The fact that he has a solid alibi proves he's innocent. It's such a relief.

No one's suspected me yet!

The hacker, whoever they are, must have been sitting in front of a computer on Wednesday evening. That rules out anyone who was at an after-school club that day . . .

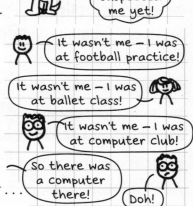

It wasn't me — I was at football practice!

It wasn't me — I was at ballet class!

It wasn't me — I was at computer club!

So there was a computer there!

Doh!

Keziah is relieved about Axel's innocence too and she's no longer annoyed with me. Phew.

She was right, as usual. As happy as I am, it also feels frustrating that every time I take two steps forward towards finding the culprit, I take another step back.

> TAKE TWO STEPS FORWARDS
> AND ONE STEP BACK
>
> DO NOT COLLECT £200
> IF YOU PASS GO

I thought I'd finally solved the mystery, but instead I'm just as confused and clueless as when I began. At least my other investigation's making more progress. I'm definitely getting closer to finding out who M.H. is . . .

That's what you think!

Gah!

In the afternoon, we do more coding exercises with Mrs Chen. We're shown an animation of a dancing cat, then we're put into pairs and have to use a coding program called Itch to make the same animation ourselves. There's loads of new lingo for us to learn.

GLOSSARY OF TERMS

Sprite – a computer graphic that may be moved on screen and manipulated as a single entity

Costumes – the different positions of a sprite

Tiles – linking parts of the command chain

Script – the narrative made by linking tiles

I'm with Axel. We choose the identical cat from a choice of different 'sprites'. We then have to choose the 'costumes' so that the cat will move into different dance positions. We copy the same ones from the animation we've been shown.

There are lots of different 'tiles'. They all have different inputs on them. 'Command tiles' say stuff like 'when the space key is pressed' or 'when this sprite is clicked'. 'Motion tiles' say stuff like 'move ten steps' or 'turn ninety degrees', although you can change the number of steps and degrees to replicate whatever dance move you want.

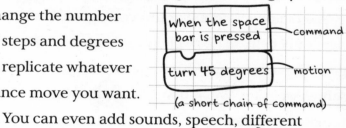

When the space bar is pressed — command

turn 45 degrees — motion

(a short chain of command)

You can even add sounds, speech, different backgrounds and other characters to create a really elaborate dance.

Hey! Woo! Yeah!

When the tiles are linked, you can make a chain of instructions. When these commands are all put together they make up the 'script', which gives us the dancing cat!

Wish I could nap. Really not in a dancing mood right now

By dragging the correct tiles and linking them in the scripts window in the right order, we replicate the dance. It's really fun!

After we've finished, we're allowed to make our own dance routines. It's so cool. You can change the music and speed everything up or slow it down or even choose new moves. We change our sprite to a dancing banana, which reminds me of the hacking mystery.

Axel's not very good at this coding stuff and needs my help, so he really wouldn't have been any good at hacking into the school website. Tina is first to finish everything.

Finished!

She's so good at this! Maybe *she* could be the hacker?! I'm all out of leads so I need at least one suspect, and Tina fits the bill.

No one's suspected me yet!

But how would she have known about the Edwards lie? She was sitting right behind us when we told Axel, that's how! I need to find out if Tina has an alibi for last night.

I told her!

'Hey, Tina,' I say casually. 'Thought I saw you in Nando's yesterday evening. Was that you?'

'Nah,' she replies. 'I was home all evening mucking about on the computer. Talking of which,' she continues, 'did you see the latest hack? So funny!'

Hmmmmm. Very suspicious indeed, and I reckon Tina would definitely be capable of decoding our original note from the bin. I'm watching you, Tina Mories . . . I'm watching you . . .

Programming the dance moves for the cat and the banana reminds me that I still need to work on my own dance moves for the opening group number. That's if the science show goes ahead. I feel mildly sick at the thought of having to remember it all. Just being in time to the

music in front of a live
audience is sending me
into a tailspin.

Huh?! Is she supposed to be doing that?

At least when it was
only me and Jake, if I
went wrong I could just style it out. With a group
number, everyone needs to be slick and in time
with each other. If one person's not on it, they
massively stand
out from the
others . . . and not
in a good way!

What's Cookie doing?

At lunch break, Keziah and I bump into Vicky
and DJ.

'How come you're in the junior school?' I ask
them. 'Anyone would think you guys prefer it here.'

'Got to drop Tayo's packed lunch off at the main
office,' says DJ. 'He left it at home.'

OK, Dorcan — your secret's safe with me!

'Any luck with De
Souza?' Vicky asks.

'Haven't had a chance

to speak to her yet,' I say.
'I haven't even seen her
around.'

Uh-oh!! Hope I don't see her around . . .

We all walk in the direction of the school office, and as though she's just heard us talking about her, Mrs De Souza appears from out of nowhere, clutching a canteen tray with her lunch on it.

Uh-oh!! I was hoping I wouldn't see them around . . .

'No time like the present!' says Vicky under her breath, prodding me in the ribs.

'Hi, Mrs De Souza!' I blurt out.

'Cookie,' she replies, 'could you open the door to my office for me, please? I could do without redecorating the walls with spaghetti bolognese and apple crumble!'

Actually, it may be an improvement on the patterned carpet and green walls

'Ha ha!' I laugh nervously. 'Good one! I'd be more than happy to oblige.'

I cringe on hearing my own words.

?!

I sound awkward and weird. As she enters the office, her pen rolls off her tray onto the floor.

Uh-oh!! I was hoping I wouldn't roll onto the floor . . .

I pick it up and put it on her desk.

'Thank you, Cookie,' she says.

Thank you, Cookie!

'That's OK!' I smile. 'Err . . . while I've got you, I was really hoping I could convince you to reinstate the science show.'

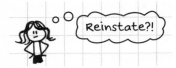

Reinstate?!

Mrs De Souza looks confused.

It turns out the show isn't cancelled after all – it's yet another Woodburn rumour! Mrs De Souza says she's very committed to the show and it's extremely important, given the school's dedication to primary science learning.

Yes . . . the number of experiments I've written up is crazy. Anyone would think I work at CERN!

'Phew!' I say. 'I'm so glad I asked you. I was scared that you might get angry.'

TRICKED YOU! I AM ANGRY!!

Last time I was in Mrs De Souza's office it was with Jake and I thought I was going to get expelled for a science experiment that had gone wrong. Long story . . .

COOKIE!

Mrs De Souza smiles and tells me that sometimes it's important to fight for what you believe in, even if it's a little bit scary.

'The suffragettes are a great example,' she says.

'Look what happened with them – they got women the vote!'

Asking if the science show is going ahead compared to being a suffragette . . . not quite the same, but I'll take the praise.

Mrs De Souza leans in towards me. 'Not many people know this,' she says in hushed tones, 'but I once got taken to the police station for protesting against the paving over of a local park to make way for a multi-storey car park and office complex. But I don't regret it – I believed in it.'

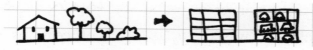

Asking if the science show is going ahead compared to protesting so the police detain you . . . not quite the same, but I'll take the praise.

'It's lovely that you tried to fight for something that you believe in, Cookie,' says Mrs De Souza, opening the door to let me out.

'Thanks so much!' I say, turning back before I exit the room. 'By the way, did the office-block development get cancelled in the end?'

'I'm afraid not – it went ahead,' sighs Mrs De Souza.

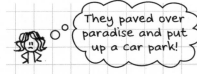
They paved over paradise and put up a car park!

 The others are waiting for me outside.

'The science show is back on!' I say triumphantly, as if it was all my doing.

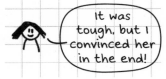
It was tough, but I convinced her in the end!

Vicky and DJ high-five me and Keziah gives me a huge hug.

'Nice one, Cookie!' says DJ.

Yay!! It feels great being in everyone's good books again.

That evening, I decide to immerse myself in a celebratory game of *Khushi's Quest*. Whoa! That's weird . . . I can see that ILC has completed the whole game and they've racked up a really high score too. They've unlocked nearly all of the achievements!

Amazing! Must be Roubi. Unless Dad's been playing late at night when he gets in from the restaurant. Odd.

Before I have the chance to think about it too much, Keziah calls.

'There's been another hack!' she says. 'Get on the school website. Now!'

I log on quick smart to see that this time Mrs De Souza's teacher profile has been tampered with.

It reads:

Julia De Souza is Woodburn Primary's award-nominated head teacher, achieving Highly Commended status in last year's Primary Teaching Awards for the category of most innovative head teacher.

Then, in an unmatching font, the website goes on to say:

She has come a long way since her rebellious youth, when her misdemeanours included being detained by the police for causing a social nuisance and protesting against a local building development.

My heart sinks. This is exactly what Mrs De Souza told *me* in her office today in *complete confidence.* I've told no one else, but now it's on the school website. And Mrs De Souza will think it's all my doing . . . I feel sick.

CHAPTER 15

The Secret Gamer

How has this happened? My palms feel clammy and my stomach knotted.

'Do you think it's true?' asks Keziah.

I pause. Should I tell Keziah about what happened in De Souza's office? Oh help. De Souza must think it's me. What will happen to me? How will I prove my innocence? I have no alibi. So much is going through my head right now.

As I'm sitting in front of the computer, an advert pops up . . .

Thinking of selling your home? Want to get the best price?

Marcus Hartnell Estate Agents can help get you a top deal.

Harvey Marcus and Benedict Hartnell have both been in the house-selling business for over twenty years and would be happy to help.

There's a picture of two suave-
looking middle-aged men in suits
grinning away.

They both have wedding rings on, which means
they must be married so probably aren't dating
Valerie. I immediately tell Keziah that we can strike

Marcus Hartnell off the
M.H. suspect list, as he
doesn't even exist!

Marcus Hartnell

Thank goodness we're no longer talking about
the hack, so I can have a bit of breathing space to
think about how to deal with this. Even though I
didn't do the latest hack (or any of them, for that
matter!), it certainly feels like I'm guilty. Mrs De
Souza trusted me with this info. How did someone
else get hold of it?
I just don't
understand.

Keziah looks up the Marcus Hartnell website on
her computer.

'Oh, yeah!' she says. 'On their homepage it says
that they're brothers-in-law. It's a small, trustworthy
family business. Look! As well as that, Mr Hartnell's
wife, Tricia Hartnell, is the office manager.

It's definitely a family affair.'

'Safe to say he's not our M.H.'

Keziah might as well be speaking gobbledygook. I'm so distracted that I hardly hear what she's saying . . .

All I want to do is clear *my* name.

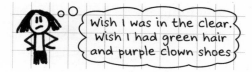

'So, Mariusz Handyman is our frontrunner, I guess,' she says. 'It seems a bit weird that he'd sign a romantic note "Mariusz Handyman", but maybe it's like an in-joke they have.'

'Yeah, I guess,' I reply. 'Errr . . . I'd better go now. I'm feeling a bit funny. Must be something I ate.' Ugh. I hate lying to Keziah.

'Are you OK?' she asks. 'What have you eaten?

Lucky you don't eat pork –
the sausage casserole at
lunchtime was really dodgy,
according to Axel.'

Keziah is vegetarian and
has never eaten meat.

'Not sure what it was,' I reply. 'I'll be fine. Just
need a lie-down, I think.'

I have to get off the phone. I won't be fine. I feel
rubbish.

'Bye,' I say and hang up.

I lie on my bed and curl
up into a ball.

How has this happened? Is it something De
Souza's said to other people too? Maybe it's one of
her standard pep talks to
students? Maybe one of
those other students did
this? Maybe she won't
just suspect me?

I was supposed to be popping over to Jake's to
practise my abysmal dance moves. Jake is going
to be at his dad's all weekend (he goes there most
weekends and every Wednesday night), so this

is our last chance to go through our
routine together before the actual show!
The actual show!!! Nooooooo!!

Noooo!!

I am dreading it.
My dances moves are
about as good as a plank
of wood's . . .

Oi – I'm a
very good
dancer, thank
you very much!

As well as not being able to do the moves, I can't
even think about them at the moment as I'm so
preoccupied with this latest turn of events. Maybe
I should have told Keziah the truth, but I can't tell
anyone or
they might
suspect me!
I mean, if I
wasn't me
then
I'd suspect
me right now!

Right, so Mrs
De Souza told
only you and you
have no alibi?

Yep

It's definitely you . . .

But you're me!

Yep, but I'm just being honest!

At Jake's, I try to act normal, but it's just not
working. All I can think of is De Souza's
face when she sees the school website.
She'll be mortified.

Noooo!!

Maybe the school are ringing my home right

now? Roubi's at politics club at the moment so Nani will most likely answer the phone. She won't understand.

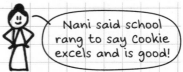

It will probably get lost in translation . . .

I have an uneasy sinking feeling in my stomach – it's kind of like a cross between a void and a washing machine.

It's the feeling you get when you know you're in trouble.

'Are you OK, Cookie?' Jake asks.

Err . . . let me think about that. Having escaped near-certain expulsion when my science experiment soaked everything within a one-metre radius, an incident that happened at

the beginning of term (long story), I'm now about to get green-seated again, but this time I'm innocent.

'Yeah, I'm fine,' I lie. 'Just thinking about my moves.'

I can't bring myself to tell Jake either. Everyone is going to think it was me! Jake's doorbell goes. Mariusz Handyman, no doubt! Probably over to 'fix the plumbing' . . . AGAIN.

We hear some animated chat from a loud voice downstairs. Whoever it belongs to is chuckling away heartily.

'Never a quiet moment in this house!' I say. 'Who's that laughing in the kitchen?'

'Who knows?' replies Jake. 'I don't know what Mum gets up to these days – she's acting more secretive than ever. Get this, she's even gone and bought a second phone, like a spy or something!'

'Or a criminal!' I say.

'Maybe she doesn't want us to see her call

activity cos we're
always taking her
phone to play games
on.' He sighs. 'So
suspicious.'

'Come on!' says Jake.
'Let's get this dance
locked down!'

For a moment, I forget about my impending
doom. It feels nice to be a normal member
of the public again, but Jake's mention of the
dance sequence brings me crashing right back
to reality . . .

Will I actually be in the science show now? Will
I even be a pupil at Woodburn Primary this time
tomorrow? How will I prove my innocence?

'Snap out of it, Cookie!'

'Huh?'

'Focus!'

Jake is right: I need to put it out of my head.

Dance moves, dance moves, dance moves. Focus.

Argggghhhhhhhh. It is no use. No matter how hard I try, my mind wanders off.

Just then, Valerie pops her head round Jake's bedroom door. A dark-haired man is standing behind her.

'Jake, you know Matteo,' says Valerie.

Now let me guess . . . Matteo with a surname beginning with H?! How many random men does Valerie know with the initials M.H.?!

'Hey, Matty,' says Jake, as the owner of the hearty laugh follows Valerie into the room and smiles at us.

'Your dinner is in the oven, Jake,' says Valerie. 'Matteo is watching you kids tonight. I have book club. Oh, and wish Matteo congratulations – he and Mariusz are finally getting married this weekend. Isn't that exciting?'

'Congratulations!' says Jake.

'Where are you guys going on honeymoon?' Valerie asks, turning to Matteo.

'Venice,' he replies.

'Ooh, lovely!' Valerie coos. 'You can go on a gondola! I read in a magazine that Venice is the third most romantic city in the world!'

'Are you marrying Mariusz who fixed the kitchen sink?' I ask.

'Yes, he is,' says Valerie. 'Mariusz recommended Matteo to us. Matteo is one of the best babysitters in town! You should tell your mum.'

'Whose surname will you take?' I interrupt.

'We'll be Mr and Mr Kowalski-Virgilio,' says Matteo.

'Double-barrelled – lovely! Very classy!' says Valerie as they leave the room. I can hear Jake's brother Will wittering away outside. 'I like double-barrelled names,' he says. 'Toby Barnett-Jones at poetry club has one. He's got a dog called Odysseus. I wonder if he has a double-barrelled surname too . . .'

So, Mariusz is in the clear. No M.H. and no hacker! Well, apart from ME as the number-one suspect, that is! I instantly feel sick again.

When I get home, I'm half expecting my parents to be waiting there, furious with me, but everything seems normal. I'm still in the clear . . . for now. Dad has gone to the restaurant and Mum has saved me dinner as everyone else has eaten already. I'm so not hungry but somehow manage to clear my plate.

There's no room for food in here with the sick, the void, the washing machine and the knot

Later that night, I'm tossing and turning in bed when I hear laughter outside. I peek out of the window just in time to see Valerie waving goodbye to a man. But I just can't make him out, as he's walking down the street to his car with his back to me. No book. Again! Ugh! If only I'd got to the window faster, I might have seen more. It's already 9.30 p.m. . . . a bit late on a school night, Valerie. I just can't sleep with this latest hack hanging over me.

HACK

Go away and leave me alone

I wander downstairs to get a glass of water, only to hear noises coming from the living room.

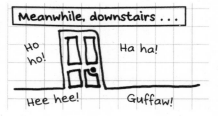

Meanwhile, downstairs . . .

Ho ho!

Ha ha!

Hee hee!

Guffaw!

Maybe Dad's just got in from the restaurant? Or it could be Roubi having a late-night snack?

I open the door to find Nani wide awake, playing *Khushi's Quest*! Huh? No way! Nani is the mystery gamer? Why hadn't I thought of that before?! Nani's always in here, sitting in front of the TV . . . I just didn't realise she might be into gaming at her age. She pats the sofa seat, grinning, and beckons me over. I join her and we snuggle up together, smiling and laughing.

We play on two-player mode late into the night.

I ask Nani what ILC stands for on the scoreboard.

KHUSHI'S QUEST
NEW HIGH SCORE
ILC 730721

She chuckles, flashes me a huge grin and says, 'I Love Cookie.' Nani is just brilliant at *Khushi's Quest* and, what's more, she helps me feel a little bit better again.

Tomorrow is a new day and I really need to make progress with my investigations. One mystery solved, two to go . . .

CHAPTER 16

Prime Suspect!

I don't even remember going to bed last night. I must have fallen asleep on the sofa gaming with

Nani and either Dad carried me upstairs when he got in or I stumbled to my bedroom half conscious.

I may be old but I'm very strong

And good at gaming!

Nani is fast asleep when I leave for school the next morning. She ain't no fool!

Thank goodness I don't have to be up . . . only a fool would game until 2 a.m. on a school night!

Meanwhile, I'm yawning my head off and finding it hard to keep my eyes open. The thought of going into school after this latest hack is hideous.

Everyone will be talking about it and I'll be sitting there trying to look all innocent.

What am I even saying!? I AM innocent. Why am I acting as though I'm guilty?

It reminds me of when we're driving in the car and the police drive behind us. Dad always says he immediately gets nervous and feels guilty even though he hasn't done anything wrong!

In the playground, before going into registration, I look out for Mrs De Souza. She and Mr Hastings often stand at the school gates, greeting students as they come in. No doubt if she's there, she'll pull

me aside to have a word and then
expel me on the spot. But she
isn't.

In assembly, I sit cross-legged on the floor in a cold
sweat, waiting for the announcement to come . . .
the announcement exposing me as a meddling,
menacing computer hacker.
But it doesn't come . . .

In class, I'm sitting in a state of constant terror.
Any moment now there'll be a knock at the door
and I'll have to go to De Souza's
office and explain myself. But
there isn't . . .

This is unbearable.

'Cookie!' Jake hisses under his breath, nudging
me in the ribs.

'Huh?' I reply, annoyed that he's nudged me so
hard.

'Well, Cookie?' Mrs Mannan asks. She's obviously
just asked me a question that I haven't heard.

'Errrrr . . . I agree?' I say, trying my luck.
Everyone laughs.

'You agree about what?' replies Mrs Mannan.

'Whatever you were saying!' I answer.

Everyone laughs.

'I was saying that you were miles away!' says Mrs Mannan.

'I agree, I was miles away!' I say, not meaning to sound cheeky but sounding totally cheeky.

Everyone laughs.

'I actually asked you what a prime number is . . .'

'A number that can only be divided by one and itself to give whole numbers,' whispers Jake.

'A number that can only be divided by one and itself to give whole numbers,' I answer, mildly annoyed that Jake told me, as I actually know what they are.

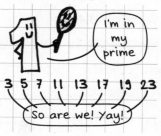

At break, Tina Mories and Clare Kelly are pinning up flyers on the school noticeboard and handing them out to people. They're for computer club. I've wanted to join computer club for a while, but it's after school on a Wednesday, which is the day Jake and his siblings usually go to his dad's, so I have full custody of Bluey.

Bluey is the cat I share with Jake. I've known her practically since she was born and I love her more than anything in the world. I've designated Wednesdays as special 'Bluey and Cookie cuddle-fest days'.

'Hey, Cookie!' says Clare, thrusting a flyer into my hand. 'You should join up – you'd like it!'

'Errr . . . thanks!' I say hesitantly, feeling very much like she thinks I'm the hacker.

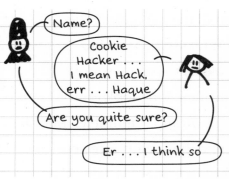

All morning I've been acting weird and guilty when there's no logic behind it at all. I'M INNOCENT!!

What's wrong with me?! Besides, I'm supposed to be the one who suspects Tina. She was home AND on the computer that Wednesday night when the school logo changed to a banana!

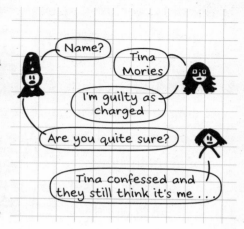

'Did you see the latest hack?' asks Tina.

This is unbearable!

'Did *you*?' I reply abruptly.

'Errr, yeah . . . that's why I was asking,' she says.

'Do you think it's true?' asks Clare.

What is this? Some kind of test? Did I see it? Do I think it's true? I *know* it's true. The head teacher told me in confidence. Why are they asking me all these questions? Hope I don't look guilty.

'Dunno,' I mumble. 'Mrs De Souza doesn't seem like the "being arrested" type,' I add.

A clever tactic . . .

1. She didn't get arrested, but if I was innocent (which I am) I wouldn't know that (although I do).

2. I am telling the truth (she *doesn't* seem like the 'being arrested' type), so even though I'm being kind of deceitful, I'm not actually lying.

I look down at the flyer and gasp in disbelief.

It has the hacked school logo on the front with the pixellated banana. Exactly the same banana image from the hack!

The trail goes hot again! The hacker *is* Tina and maybe even Clare too!

'Who made this flyer?' I ask.

'We knocked them up on the computer yesterday lunchtime,' says Clare. 'Do you like them?'

'Where did you get that banana image?' I ask.

'Don't you recognise it?' says Tina.

190

Recognise it?! Of course I recognise it! Is this still a test?!

'We copied it from the school website after the hack on Wednesday,' she continues.

Hmmmmm.

'Funny flyer, huh?' says Clare.

Back of flyer

I look at the back . . .

It's pretty impressive for

- Wanna be able to change the school logo to a banana?
- Wanna know your bytes from your bites?
- GET WITH THE PROGRAM! JOIN COMPUTER CLUB NOW!
- Your computer needs you . . .

something that was designed on a computer in lunch hour. They've definitely got good computer design skills, although I'm not sure about the 'Want to know your bytes from your bites?' line!

Wanna know a mouse from a mouse?

Without Computer Club I almost kept this in a cage!

Luckily, thanks to Woodburn's Computer Club, I now know this is not an animal.

'Yeah, it's good,' I say, 'but where were you after school yesterday?'

They look at me as though I'm mad.

'We were both at chess club,' says Tina, bemused.

Ugh! Good alibi. Back to square one.

This is utter madness. Tina and Clare wander off, clearly thinking I'm crazy. I feel as though I *am* going crazy. What is De Souza doing? Why hasn't she expelled me yet? The waiting and not knowing is driving me insane!

I spot Mrs De Souza walking across the playground. I have to get to her first and explain. I have to clear my name and put myself out of this abject misery. I have to take control of the situation.

I race over to her, loudly protesting my innocence. At first, she's very confused . . .

. . . . then she bursts out laughing.

'I didn't think it was you for one moment, Cookie! I often tell that story when I'm giving students an empowerment talk. It's quite a good one, isn't it? I'd actually forgotten I'd even mentioned that to you!'

Charming.

'The so-called hacker would have to have better computing skills than the Key Stage 2 computer curriculum!'

Double charming.

I feel a bit embarrassed now.

'It definitely couldn't have been a nine-year-old!' she says. 'Besides, students aren't the only ones who know about my brush with the police! I even mentioned it to Mr Hastings the other day when I was giving him some self-motivation tips.

'I'm quite the celebrity for standing up for my morals and sticking to my guns, even when faced

193

with the long arm of the law! At the time, I even gave a comment to the local paper!'

Wow, you're the lady who was against the car park — can I have your autograph?

Err . . . why, yes, of course!

She scuttles off across the playground, still smiling away to herself at my obvious distress over the whole situation. Triple charming.

I do look innocent!

Hang on . . . did she say Mr Hastings knew? Interesting . . . very interesting . . .

Suddenly it all starts to make sense. *He's* the one who wanted the science show cancelled. *He's* older and has the necessary computing skills.

Mr Hastings MUST be the Woodburn Hacker!!!!

CHAPTER 17

Hastings the Hacker?!

I need to get to the bottom of this. The whole thing is turning into an obsession. At least I'm no longer about to be expelled for being the hacker. Plus, the science show is going ahead, which is another positive. I still feel the need to figure out who the culprit is, though, for some strange reason. Could it really be Hastings? I won't be able to relax until I know the truth . . .

It has to be Hastings. There's no one else it could be. I need to find Jake and Keziah and get their thoughts on the matter. I spot Keziah on the far side of the playground with Axel. He's showing her some invisible-ink messages.

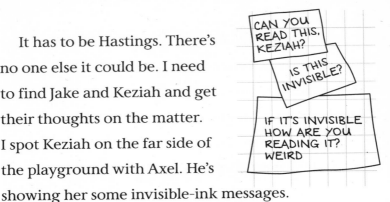

I walk over to them. 'These ones were done with lemon juice,' he says, 'and these ones with milk.'

'Hey!' I interrupt. 'Have either of you seen Jake?'

'I think he went to the library to give a book back,' says Keziah. 'He said he forgot to return it last week.'

'We'll come with you to find him,' offers Axel. 'I need to put these on the radiator in the library.'

We head inside the main building and bump into Jake in the corridor. He's coming out of the library.

Axel disappears off to dry his invisible-ink messages and I tell Keziah and Jake all about Hastings. They aren't convinced.

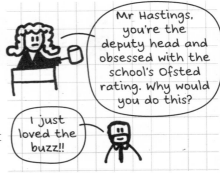

'Why would he change his *own* teacher profile and say that he's engaged to Miss Rai?' asks Jake.

'Hmmmm.' I bite my lip uncertainly. That's a good question. I hadn't thought about that.

'Maybe to cover his tracks?' suggests Keziah.

'Yeah!' I agree. Good explanation, Keziah!

Jake still isn't convinced. To be honest, I'm not sure any of us really are, but it's all we have to go on.

'I think we need more evidence!' says Jake. 'I'm not sure that the motive of cancelling the science show really adds up – especially as the science show hasn't even been cancelled.'

Break is nearly over, so we decide to do some investigating at lunchtime. Maybe question him . . . or follow him around.

Jake suggests looking in Hastings' office in case there are any clues or evidence that point towards him.

At lunchtime, we scoff our food as quickly as possible.

Once we've finished, we all feel a bit queasy.

On the verge of vomiting or at the very least indigestion, we head towards Hastings' office.

'We need a plan!' says Jake.

'Do you think we could sneak into his office?' I suggest.

'I could be the look-out,' offers Keziah, 'and cough loudly if I see him coming?'

'It's too risky,' replies Jake. 'We'll be in real trouble if he finds us.'

He's right. I really don't want to go through life continuously on the verge of expulsion . . .

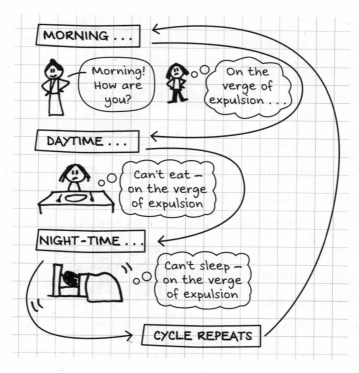

We decide that we need an actual reason to go to his office. We try to think of some good excuses to get us in there . . .

1. 'We made you a Best Deputy Head Teacher certificate and wanted to present it to you in person.'
   TOO WEIRD!

2. 'The caretaker sent us to check if your heating's working.'

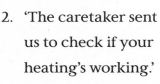

   WHY WOULD THE CARETAKER NOT CHECK HIMSELF?

3. Write his name on a random bit of stationery and say, 'We found your stapler on the floor in the corridor, sir, and came to return it.'
   HE WOULD RECOGNISE THAT THE STAPLER WITH HIS NAME ON WASN'T HIS AND SMELL A RAT.

As we're loitering outside Hastings' office, deciding which plan to go with, he suddenly appears from behind us.

'Looking for me?' he chirps. 'You'd better come in!'

Wowzers! Gaining entry was soooooo easy. Hastings is having one of his good days. He's chipper and upbeat. Phew. Every now and then he literally has a personality transplant – there's no rhyme or reason to it. It's like a lottery . . . but at least we're safe today.

'What can I do for you?' he asks.

Uh-oh. It might help if we *actually* had a plan!

'We found your ruler on the floor!' says Keziah, pulling a ruler out from her bag.

'How do you know it's mine?' he asks, confused.

'I thought I saw you with it once!' she says.

'A case of mistaken identity, I believe,' he replies, bemused.

'Easy mistake to make,' I add, trying to act all casual. 'We also

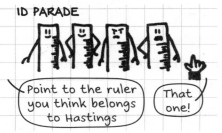

wanted to tell you a bit about the new, improved science show,' I say, 'so you could put it on the school website.'

At the mention of the science show his face goes red and he suddenly looks as if he's going to get angry. But then, weirder than weird, he does a double take and turns all nice. So strange!

'Ah, you need Mrs Chen for that,' he says. 'She's an admin for the school website.' He smiles, then winks at Jake.

Odd.

'Besides, my computer has been on the blink for

the last couple
of weeks.
Computers
really don't
agree with me.

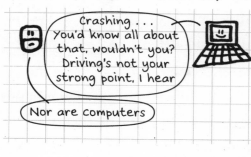

I can never get the blasted things to work! They're

always
crashing
on me.
'Computing is
like another
language to

me!' He laughs.

Not into
the science
show? Not into
computing?
Are you at

the right school, Mr Hastings? I look at his desk.

Next to the computer is a book titled *Computing*

for Dummies. Is this all a ruse to make him look

innocent and incapable of hacking? Hastings has

loads of books on his
desk. Most of them
are self-help books . . .

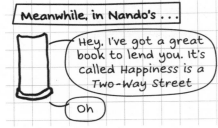

There's also
a folder marked 'Miss Rai'. That's the name of
the Reception teacher he was in Nando's with.

Hmmmm.

Meanwhile, in Nando's . . .

Hey, I've got a great book to lend you. It's called Happiness is a Two-Way Street

Oh

Maybe
Miss Rai *is* his
girlfriend after
all?

'You should really go and see Mrs Chen,' he
says. 'She can pop it all on the school website for
you. Actually, while you're at it, can you drop this
envelope off to Miss Rai
in Reception?'

Dear Miss Rai,
You make
me feel like
I've won the
lottery.
Winner
winner,
chicken
dinner! — M.H.
xx

Miss Rai!
PRIVATE

Envelope? I wonder
what's in it. Maybe it's a
love letter from Hastings
to Miss Rai?

I notice a photo in a frame on his desk. I wonder
if he has a wife and kids. I need to see the front of
it. Or maybe Miss Rai is in it? I grab the ruler off
Keziah and fling it under the desk. Jake and Keziah

look at me as
though I'm mad.

'Oops! Dropped the ruler!' I say. 'So clumsy. Let me just get it back!'

I go to grab the ruler and see that the picture in the frame is of him leaning against a car bonnet?!!

'Nice car!' I say. 'But I thought you didn't drive?'

'Don't believe the nonsense you read on the school website.' He laughs. 'It was my nephew who failed his driving test seven times, not me! Fake news! Next, you'll be telling me the school logo *is* a banana, right, Jakey?!' He winks at Jake again.

Jakey?!!!!

'Umm, right . . .' says Jake, a bit perplexed at this new interest in him from Hastings.

My brain is whirring at 100 miles per hour.

As soon as school is finished, I race to the staff car park to look for the car from Hastings' photo. I find it with ease and check out the number plate.

I pull my notepad out of my rucksack to cross-check it. Unbelievably, it matches.

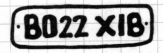

Although Hastings may not be the hacker, it's looking more and more likely that he is M.H. . . . It would certainly explain why he's being so chummy with Jake. Could Mr Hastings really be Valerie's new boyfriend?!! Surely not? If this is true, Jake will NOT be happy.

CHAPTER 18

Science Museum

Saturday morning and I'm woken up by Bluey jumping onto my bed and snuzzling me. Pure bliss! Her soft, warm body makes me want to curl up and go back to sleep. Roubi must have let her in. These days, Jake and his

Jake's deserted me all weekend — I guess I'll have to hang out with his weird neighbour again!

siblings are with his dad most weekends, so I often get Bluey all to myself. Yay!

Reluctantly, I get up and wander downstairs in my pyjamas to make myself some cereal. Roubi goes to pass me the milk from the fridge, and as she does so the computer exhibition leaflet flutters off

the fridge door and onto

the floor as if to say

'Visit me, Cookie!'

She picks it up and glances at it.

'Hey! This expires today!'

'No way!' I reply. 'It's supposed to be really good.
Do you wanna go?'

Roubi says she can't as she's off to visit Nahid for
the weekend. Gah. I ask Mum, who says she has to
drop Roubi off. Double gah. So I ask Dad, who says

he has to go shopping for
supplies for the restaurant.
Triple gah!!!!

Typical. Just
typical.

In a huff, I decide

to eat my cereal on the sofa in the living room. Nani
is already in there, gaming. She's turning into an
addict. I'm only allowed one hour of screen time

a day. She's
probably had
an hour already
and it's not even
8 a.m.!

That's when it comes to me . . . Nani! NANI! NANIIIIIIIIIIIII!!!!! My saviour! If you need something done, go to the top!

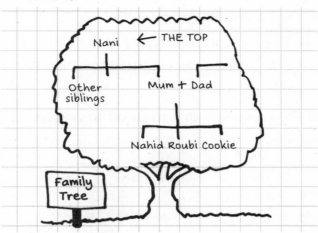

I wave the leaflet in her face and point to the gaming pics.

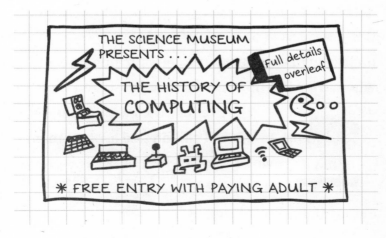

'*Cholo!*' I say to Nani, using my limited Bengali.

cho + lo
cholo = Bengali for 'let's go'

'*Ha!*' says Nani, chuckling. (That means 'yes' in Bengali.)

ha = Bengali for 'yes'

She then grins and says 'yes please' using her very limited English.

Yay!!! I love it when a plan comes together. Mum packs us one of her famous snack bags so we have enough food in case we get stuck in a hostage situation.

We're in a siege — we could be here for weeks!

Don't worry . . . I have enough food to feed 100 people for months!

When we leave the house, I notice a fresh bouquet of flowers in the vase on Jake's windowsill where the M.H. flowers had been.

Look at us!

Don't just stick us on a windowsill and take us for granted!

They're red roses with a massive bright red ribbon tied around them, which is why they catch my eye. M.H. has struck again!

Mwah ha ha!

As we walk down the road, I turn back to look again. Is that M.H.'s car I can see parked not too far from Jake's house? I need to stop thinking about all this and just enjoy the exhibition.

FOCUS!!

Nani's never been on the Tube before, but I show her the map and the key displaying all the different-coloured train lines. I point to the station we need to get to. She works out our route and navigates us there in no time at all. Nani would be a brilliant code-breaker!

'Scuse me, ma'am, I'm recruiting for MI5 and I could not help but notice you with that Tube map. Do you have a minute?

The exhibition is SO fascinating. Although the first proper computer was invented by Charles Babbage in the mid-1800s, there are early computation tools that date back to over 2,000 years BC. This blows my mind! The first was called the Sumerian abacus and used pebbles and lines

Huh?! I paid a fortune for this and it's just pebbles and sand!!

drawn in the sand to do calculations.

Early computation was pretty much just calculating answers to maths problems. The Chinese abacus came a bit later, in the 2nd century BC, and is still used today, particularly by children.

Then, in the 3rd century BC, Archimedes used the mechanical principle of balance to calculate things like the number of grains of sand in the universe. Extra mind-blowing! I can't believe someone could've been so smart over 2,000 years ago when there were no computers or anything!

Although I don't really understand the mechanical principle of balance, one fascinating thing I do learn is that Archimedes discovered that when you put an object in a container full to the brim with water, the amount of water that spills out is the same as the volume of the object. Apparently, he discovered this when he got in the bath, and afterwards he ran naked through the streets of Syracuse shouting 'Eureka!'

I also learn that the earliest mechanical analogue computer has been dated to around 100 BC and was called the Antikythera mechanism. It was designed to calculate the positions of stars and was found washed up on the edge of the Aegean Sea.

Here's another thing that totally blows my mind . . . almost all modern-day computers and computer-based devices use  the binary system, which consists of only TWO numbers – 0s and 1s! How weird! It's amazing to think that a code that just uses 0s and 1s can give a really complex set of instructions.

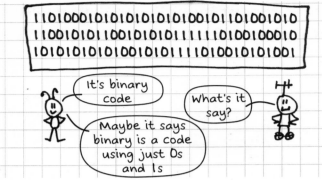

After getting my head around how to write numbers in binary, I show Nani the section of the exhibition about Ada Lovelace. Nani smiles. I like to think she's as obsessed with her as I am, but I'm not sure she is.

After we've whizzed through the historical bit, we spend AGES in the gaming section. We play *Pong*, *Space Invaders*, *Pac-Man*, *Paperboy*, *Donkey Kong* and loads of old classics, followed by some more modern ones, including an incredible virtual-reality experience.

There are other immersive and interactive games too, including a driving one and a skiing one. Nani seems to love motorbike racing. Who knew?!

At 6 p.m. the museum is closing and we have to leave. We've had such a brilliant time.

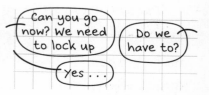

We've been in there for eight hours – from opening time right through to closing! I'd been looking forward to eating in the museum restaurant, but that's out of the question now. Luckily, I don't mind at all because it's been so much fun. Instead, we polish off the remaining contents of Mum's snack bag, which is pretty good going considering how much there was inside it to begin with!

Nani and I link arms.

Once we're back in Ealing and nearly home, we pass an Indian restaurant and Nani

can read the sign because the Bengali translation is written beneath the English.

'Garam Masala Restaurant,' she says. 'Let's go!'

'*Cholo!*' I say, as we haven't had a proper dinner yet. We head inside.

Garam Masala
গরম মসলা
Restaurant
রেষ্টরেণ্ট

I'm about to say, 'A table for two, please!' but Nani beats me to it and asks for one in Bengali! She's quite the charmer with the waiters and they quickly warm to her cheekiness.

She orders loads of delicious food for us in Bengali, and it turns out our waiter's parents were born in a village not too far from hers. SMALL WORLD!!

Small world

She has all the staff entertained with her stories
from back home, and they translate any bits I can't
understand.
We're
having a
blast!

She says she finished Khushi's Quest in a few days

Is that true?

Yes, that's my nani!

I tell them
all that my dad has an Indian restaurant as well and
it turns out that one of the waiters
has actually eaten there. EVEN
SMALLER WORLD!!

Small world

We eat till we're totally stuffed. We don't even
manage to finish all our food, as Mum's snack bag
already did a good job of filling us up, so the waiters
bag up the rest of it for us in takeaway containers.

That's tomorrow's lunch sorted – yay!

That's less cooking for me tomorrow – yay!

Walking out into the crisp night
air with our arms linked again,
we feel so happy (or *khushi* in
Bengali!).

খুশি

KHUSHI

I've had such a lovely day not worrying about

hackers or M.H. but just having pure, simple fun.

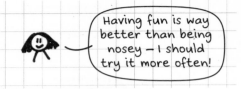

As we walk past the Nando's on the corner, I catch the eye of someone familiar through the window. I do a double take but she ducks down behind her menu, pretending she hasn't seen me. I'm sure it's Valerie.

Annoyingly, I can't quite make out who she's sitting with . . .

It all happens so

quickly that I wonder whether it definitely is Valerie or not. I only saw her for a split second. Maybe it was someone similar-looking . . .

I notice a car parked nearby. A car with a 'Teachers Do it Better' bumper sticker.

The car's number plate matches the one I saw in the school car park yesterday.

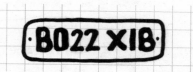

It's the same car as the one I saw outside Jake's house that night . . . and the same as the car in the photo in Mr Hastings' office . . . This car belongs to Martin Hastings . . . or should I say, this car belongs to M.H.!? All my suspicions are confirmed. Mr Hastings is Valerie's secret boyfriend!

CHAPTER 19

The First Half

Lying in bed that night, I just can't sleep. I'm SO confused. Should I tell Jake? If I do tell him, he'll be fuming.

> Thanks a bunch, Cookie – why are you telling me this? I HATE YOU!

But if I *don't* tell him, he'll also be fuming . . .

> Thanks a bunch, Cookie – why didn't you tell me this? I HATE YOU!

It's a 'catch-22' situation where you can't win no matter what you choose, so either way you lose.

> Hello and welcome to Lucky Numbers. Throw 1 to 3 and you lose, throw 4 to 6 and you also lose. Our first contestant is Marian.

> Oh.

My dad's always using the phrase 'catch-22'.
Apparently, it comes from a famous book called
Catch-22, which he read at high
school – he even wrote an essay
about it! Imagine writing a book
where the title becomes a phrase
used in everyday life.

Hmm . . . this is a mysterious mystery

I'm still confused! I hear laughter from outside.
I tiptoe over to the window, making sure that I duck
down out of sight. Tentatively,
I pull back the curtain and
peer round the edge. I almost
don't want to look . . . but at
the same time I do!

I don't wanna see . . .

. . . but maybe I do . . .

Like I say, I'm confused.
I take a peek. And, just in case there'd been any
doubt at all in my mind, I see it myself with my
own eyes: Mr Hastings, in broad daylight . . . well,
actually in broad moonlight . . . well, actually in
broad yellow lamplight.
Mr Hastings and
Valerie are TOGETHER
underneath the lamppost
outside Jake's house!!!!!

This is nice

Hope Jake can't see out of the window

YUCK!!

He's stroking her hair . . . YUCK!!

She moves a bit of fluff off his stubble . . . YUCK!!

They giggle, gazing into each other's eyes . . . YUCK!!

I can't watch. But I can't *not* watch either. I'm totally and utterly confused!!!! Thankfully they go into Jake's house, so I don't *have to* watch any more. Phew!!

AAAAAARGHHHHHH!!! MR HASTINGS IS IN JAKE'S HOUSE!!! While the cat's away . . .

. . . and the cat is literally away, snuggled up right here on my lap. Cuddling Bluey and listening to her gently purr away, I finally fall asleep.

The rest of the weekend goes in a flash. I spend all of Sunday trying to get my dance moves locked down for Monday's science show. I don't tell anyone about my discovery last night. I'm the only one who knows.

Focus. Dance moves. The problem with the dance is that it's not just remembering which moves come when to the music; I often miss out the odd move and suddenly I'm one step out of sync with the others. Everyone goes down and I go up; everyone goes up and I go down.

I stick out like a sore thumb.

Some people can dance so naturally, but to me it's like

the moves are all in code. Hang on . . . code! And that's when I crack it!! I've got an idea! My dancing problems could well be over, but I'll need Tina Mories' help . . .

I find Tina first thing on Monday morning and explain my idea to her. She likes it and says she'll tell Mrs Chen, who loves it and says she'll tell Vicky, who thinks it's a great idea and says Tina can use her laptop at rehearsals straight after school to make it happen!!

Always happy to help!

Once the school bell goes for the day, everyone is so excited. There's a real buzz in the air. We all get into costume to do a quick dress run of the whole show. Jake and I check that everybody is dancing in time during the opening number, which they totally are. Jake is confused when I watch from the front instead of actually taking part, but I have no time to explain.

Huh?

Keziah and Axel, who are stage-managing everything, have loads to remember – lighting, microphones, props and so on – but they're doing a great job.

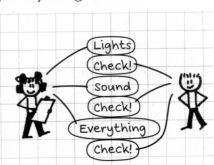

Lights
Check!
Sound
Check!
Everything
Check!

The whole thing is being
filmed for the school website
and it looks really impressive
blown up on a huge screen at
the back of the stage. It's like
being at Wembley Arena or
something!

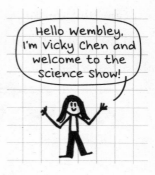

Everything has totally come together. It's both
entertaining AND informative –
just what Mrs Chen and the
teaching staff wanted.

At the end of the dress run, we all go onstage
to take our bows. The whole cast
and crew are so pleased with how
it's gone. We cheer, high-five
and group hug in our various
costumes.

People are dressed up as all sorts of different
things, from Einstein – complete with crazy white
hair – to scientists in lab
coats with goggles and multi-
coloured wigs. There are
even people dressed up as test
tubes and giant lightbulbs.

Out of sheer happiness, I throw my Ada Lovelace wig into the air and it gets caught in the lighting rig. Everyone laughs.

We all chatter away excitedly and Tina Mories (dressed as American computer scientist Grace Hopper!) bounds over to let me know that everything is sorted for my cunning plan. Yay! No dancing for me!

As if he knows something's up, Jake asks me if I'm OK with the dance. Just as I'm about to explain my plan to him, parents and audience members start filing into the hall. I see Valerie talking to Mr Hastings and quickly stand in the way to block them from Jake's view.

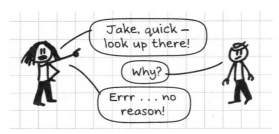

'Can you see my wig?' I say, trying to create a

diversion just as
it falls back down
onto the stage.

Lucky it didn't catch fire up there.

'Got it,' says Jake, catching
it for me as the curtain comes
down, ready for us to take
our first positions.

Everybody's parents are sitting and waiting in
the audience. I can see that even Nahid has come
back with Roubi from uni to watch, but I guess

you could say
Nani came the
furthest – all
the way from
Bangladesh!!!

The seniors do a
quick introduction,
with Vicky at the
helm, of course.

Then the first half
begins. I duck out of the dance number, but Tina
has brilliantly programmed in a dancing sprite to

replace me on the big screen, just like we learnt in coding class. It does the moves from the dance routine flawlessly and in sync. She's also put in sprites of all the other people helping out with the show, like Keziah and Axel.

The sprites' heads even change every few moves to those of various famous scientists!

And facts about each of the scientists appear on the screen . . .

1. Einstein worked at the Swiss patent office where the Toblerone chocolate bar was patented. He also hated haircuts!

2. Katherine Johnson (a brilliant American mathematician who was critical to the success of NASA's first space flight) started high school at

just ten years old – three years earlier than she was supposed to! Her first application to work at NASA was rejected . . . she applied again the following year and made it in!

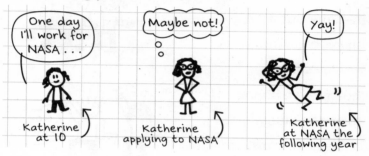

3. Marie Curie, a French physicist and chemist, worked in a shed and discovered TWO new elements in the periodic table!

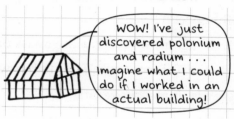

The audience are loving it – they're all applauding and laughing away. The next performance is all about how coding is responsible for so many of the things we take for granted in everyday life.

On the giant screen at the back of the stage, the word 'coding' appears. in many different forms, including Morse code, semaphore, Braille and even Bengali!

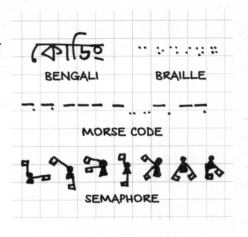

I can see from the wings that Nani grins when she spots the Bengali. If we thought the dress run had gone well, this performance is off the scale!

I go and find Tina backstage to thank her. She's deleting the sprite that she made on Vicky's laptop.

'Well done!' I say. 'That was amazing! You really are a computing genius!'

'Awww, thanks!' She grins. 'No rest for the wicked, though. Gotta go and be Grace Hopper now!'

She leaves me with Axel and Keziah, who are busy running the show. I go to close Vicky's laptop and catch a glimpse of a small icon of a banana next to a folder marked 'PRIVATE'. And suddenly everything falls into place . . .

Hack numbers: 1 & 2

Target: Mrs Chen and Mr Hastings

Motive: Revenge – Vicky was angry when Mrs Chen told her off in front of everyone at the science-show rehearsals. She was really embarrassed and even cried. Mr Hastings had wanted to cancel the science show and Vicky was mad at both Mr Hastings and Mrs Chen.

Background info: Vicky was in the car park right behind me when I overheard the end of the conversation between Chen and Hastings about failing chemistry exams and driving tests!

Hack number: 3

Target: Mr Edwards

Motive: More revenge

Background info: Vicky heard me setting the trap for Axel in rehearsals when I lied about Mr Edwards's hair falling out. She told me at the time to stop gossiping!

Hack number: 4

Target: Miss Rai

Motive: Even more revenge

Background info: This was a rumour based on Axel's original sighting of Rai and Hastings in Nando's. We know from Roubi that by the time the rumour had reached the secondary school, it had been grossly exaggerated!

Hack number: 5

Target: Mrs De Souza

Motive: Yet more revenge

Background info: Vicky was outside De Souza's office listening in to see if the science show was to be saved when De Souza told me about her brush with the law!

Not only did Vicky have all the info and a mock-up of the school logo Photoshopped with a banana, but Mrs Chen is an admin for the school website. Vicky could easily have made the changes from her home computer without actually having to 'hack' anything. No computing skills necessary.

As Vicky Chen rushes backstage in a lab coat, clutching her clipboard, I'm totally dumbstruck. I look at her, taking it all in in broad daylight . . . I mean, indoor evening light . . . I mean, backstage with hardly any light. My head is in a whirr. It all seems so obvious now. Vicky Chen is the Woodburn Hacker!

CHAPTER 20

The Show!

Vicky doesn't seem to notice that I can't stop staring at her, wide-eyed and speechless. Yes, me . . . speechless!

> That Cookie is so odd. Oh well, at least she's shut up for once! I'll enjoy it while I can!

I try to say something, but nothing comes out . . .

> Why is my speech bubble empty?

'Hurry up!' says Vicky, shoving a microphone into my hand, a wig onto my head and bundling me onstage. 'You're on, Little Miss Lovelace!'

Me, wearing Ada Lovelace wig

> How can I say my lines if I'm speechless?

Jake's already onstage doing his bit as Charles Babbage. Looking out at the audience, I feel stunned. I can see Keziah's dads, Jake's mum and the whole of my family too. All eyes are on me.

I thought this would be fine compared to remembering the dance moves, but maybe I thought too soon . . .

> Arms up . . .

> Wrong bit, you're Ada Lovelace!

What if I open my mouth and blurt out everything about Vicky Chen? It's all I can think about right now.

> A lady with both arts and science skills . . .

> Ada Lovelace?

> No – Vicky Chen! Not only a drama queen but THE WOODBURN HACKER!

Luckily, I don't reveal anything. I somehow manage to get through our act without messing it up . . . but only just.

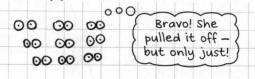

> Bravo! She pulled it off – but only just!

I'm nowhere near as good as I was in the dress

run. I even manage to forget to take my chair offstage with me . . .

Poor Keziah has to go on and retrieve it and somehow manages to get a standing ovation from her dads!!

Backstage, people are rushing around frantically with their props and outfits, but I'm still in a daze.

Keziah comes back with my chair.

'You OK, Cookie?'

'Not really,' I reply.

I need to get it all off my chest and there's no

time like the present.
So I take a deep breath,
open my mouth and tell
Keziah everything.

I tell her all about
the hacks, the identity of the hacker, her motive,
her methods, the lot. I decide I may as well reveal

M.H.'s identity
too while I'm at
it. Everything
comes out in
one go!

Bottling up these secrets was just no good for me.
As I'm spilling the beans, Tina joins us and listens in.
She and Keziah agree that it all makes total sense.

Then,
from out of
nowhere, Axel

comes flying over like
Superman and dives
at me, rugby-tackling
me to the ground,
knocking my wig off
and dishevelling me.

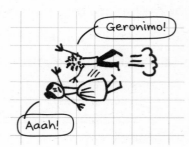

'Got it!' he yells, unplugging the battery pack from my microphone.

'Oi!' I shout. 'What are you doing?! I could have hurt myself if these petticoats hadn't broken my fall!'

These petticoats are like a crash mat!

'Your mic was still on,' explains Axel. 'Everyone heard everything you said!'

'*Everyone?*'

'Yep.'

'*Everything?*'

'Afraid so. Hastings, Chen, Jake's mum, Vicky . . .'

'OK,' I say. 'I don't need the names of every person in the school hall!'

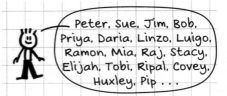

Peter, Sue, Jim, Bob, Priya, Daria, Linzo, Luigo, Ramon, Mia, Raj, Stacy, Elijah, Tobi, Ripal, Covey, Huxley, Pip . . .

EVERYONE heard EVERYTHING!! What a disaster!!! Why do these things always happen to me? What are the chances?! Vicky will hate me now . . . and as for Jake, I don't think I can even face him. I just want the ground to swallow me up.

Where did Cookie go?

I'm in here!

The ground — it swallowed me up!

'Do you think Mr Hastings is having an affair with Miss Rai as well as Jake's mum?' asks Axel.

'Certainly not!' snaps Mrs Chen. 'He's her mentor. He gives her appraisals and helps her out with school affairs. That is all!'

She then turns to a

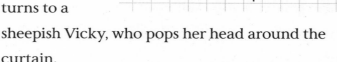

sheepish Vicky, who pops her head around the curtain.

'And have *you* got anything to say for yourself, young lady?'

A teary Vicky confesses to everything on the spot, and suddenly I feel like I'm in an episode of *Scooby-Doo*!

Vicky explains that she was really frustrated that her mum was so obsessed with science and not interested in her love of the arts. She says she'd only offered to help with the school science show in the first place to impress her mum.

The next thing I know, it turns from *Scooby-Doo* into a schmaltzy daytime soap opera.

Mrs Chen declares how proud she is of Vicky and says that she thinks her love of the arts is a fantastic thing. In fact, that's why she thought Vicky would be great at organising the science show.

'After all,' says Mrs Chen, 'creativity is vital to science. Advances in science are all to do with thinking outside the box and challenging perceived wisdom. In fact, arts and science go hand in hand – as the science show is proving.'

It's all very touching, and just as I feel a group hug coming on, Jake and DJ – who have been showing off dance moves to each other outside – bound in, unaware of all the drama that's unfolded.

'Guys!' says DJ. 'The second half's about to begin!'

Everyone gasps and people start running around

frantically, gathering their props and costumes and getting into show mode again.

'OK, everybody,' says Mrs Chen, clapping her hands. 'It's been fantastic so far – don't let us down by forgetting to do the second half!'

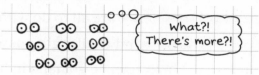

Even though this massive bombshell has just been dropped, there's no time to pause for thought. Mrs Chen gives Vicky a huge hug and laughs.

'And I gotta say, I'm so proud of all you senior-school helpers! Good job!'

'But Vicky, don't think you're off the hook that easily – that hacking stunt was not a clever one.'

Uh-oh . . . looks like Vicky's going to be grounded from now until next year's science show.

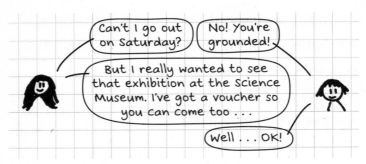

The second half goes down really well – even better than the first half. We end up getting a heartfelt standing ovation from the audience. The crowd are whistling and going wild, and Mrs De Souza gives the cast and crew a huge bunch of flowers.

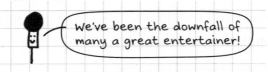

All in all, it's been a huge success . . . despite my on-mic revelations!

We've been the downfall of many a great entertainer!

On the walk home, we laugh about what Dad calls the half-time entertainment. Nani and I walk arm in arm the entire way and Mum says that Nani's really proud of me.

She tells me that when Nani was at school, although she was very bright, she only managed to finish her primary education. In some countries, like Bangladesh, education is a privilege and lots of people don't have access to it. One day I'll put my education to good use and make Nani even prouder of me.

The week after the show, Nani goes back to Bangladesh, though not before I've given her my old Z-Box 2. After Jake's mum bought him the brand-new Z-Box 3 Pro as a 'guilt gift', he offered me his old Z-Box 3! This means that Nani and I can play games over the Internet and even message each other in a mix of English, Bengali and lots of emojis! Our very own code!

I'm very khushi ☺ ♡
খুব
✗ ✗ ✗

Jake's slowly coming to terms with the fact that his mum is seeing Mr Hastings. He switches from finding the whole thing really cringey to laughing hysterically as though it's hilarious!! I'm actually quite surprised. I thought he'd be fuming! Maybe it's just a coping mechanism.

Worst part isn't Hastings, but no more guilt gifts!

But I've learnt now that people can surprise you at every turn.

Keziah enjoyed her standing ovation for moving the chair and reckons she may go for a speaking part in the next Woodburn Primary drama production!

I even saw Vicky Chen reading a book on Ada Lovelace the other day on the green. Wonders will never cease!

And as for Nani . . . to think I ever thought she was boring! I'm so glad she's in my life now. I just love her to bits. We have the best benglish-emoji chats these days!!

People aren't always what they seem on the surface. Everyone has more to them than meets the eye . . . hidden depths, complexities and secrets. In some cases you discover the truth and in others

I guess you just never know. Keziah and I still wonder what happened under the bleachers at the local football club . . .

I smile to myself as I finish the last bag of Bombay mix that Nani brought over with her, and spot Dorcan walking down the street. Don't worry, DJ – your secret's safe with me.

APPENDIX

HOW TO MAKE YOUR OWN CODE WHEEL, COOKIE-STYLE!

Materials

A pair of scissors   A pencil

A rubber – in case you make any mistakes!

A circle to draw around – I used a large tumbler, but you could use an empty hummus tub or a small bowl, anything that fits the bill – just make sure it's not too small.

Two pieces of thin card or paper →

A split-pin paper fastener

Method

Draw around your circle on one of the pieces of card.

Then cut out the circle using the scissors.

Fold your circle five times, so you have thirty-two sections.

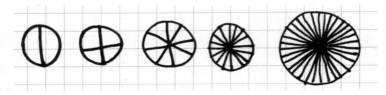

Then, write a letter at the edge of each section. Start with A and go all the way through to Z.

ABC ⟶ XYZ

In the remaining six spaces put a question mark, an exclamation mark, an @ symbol, a hashtag, a comma and a full stop.

? ! @ # , ·

Cut the end of the second piece of card so it's square. Take your paper fastener and fasten your circular piece of card to the middle of the square piece of card.

Around the edges of your circle, write the alphabet again so that each letter has the same letter or punctuation mark directly above it.

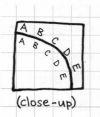

(close-up)

Set your code by rotating the circular piece of card so that the letter at the top corresponds to a different letter or symbol on the square piece of card. So, for example, you could set the code to Circle E = Square A.

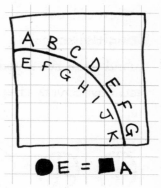

● E = ■ A

Using this code, FIEH can be decoded to BEAD.

This version of the code wheel means that the two languages we're using are 'Circle' and 'Square', so when you write your message you need to say whether it's written in 'Circle' or 'Square'.

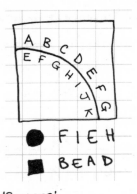

Results

You've now made your own code wheel! See if it works by decoding the following message . . .

The code we're using is SQUARE A = CIRCLE J and the message below is written in CIRCLE.

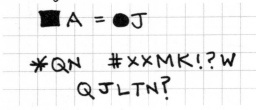

Conclusion

Nobody can read your secret messages apart from people who have the code wheel.

Now try writing your own coded messages and see if your friends can decode them! Here's a key to help you. You don't have to just use the alphabet

to represent your letters – you can also use little
pictures or symbols, like those shown below.

A	⋈		N	◨	
B	⋈		O	😊	
C	⋈		P	🙂	
D	⋈		Q	🐭	
E	◉		R	🍎	
F	🌀		S	🍌	
G	△		T	🍐	
H	▽		U	♡	
I	○		V	♣	
J	●		W	♠	
K	ψ		X	🐱	
L	⊤⊤		Y	🐶	
M	⊘		Z	🐭	

HOW TO MAKE YOUR OWN INVISIBLE-INK MESSAGES, COOKIE-STYLE!

Materials

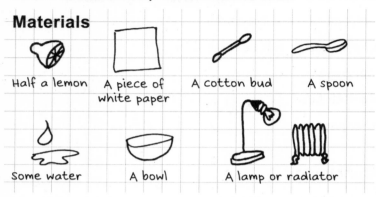

Half a lemon   A piece of white paper   A cotton bud   A spoon

Some water   A bowl   A lamp or radiator

Method

Squeeze some lemon juice into a bowl and add a few drops of water.

Mix this with the spoon.

Dip your cotton bud into the mixture and write a message on the white paper.

Wait for the lemon juice to dry. Your message will become completely invisible.

Wow!! Where did it go?

Results

When your piece of paper is put on a radiator or held close to a lightbulb (or other heat source) the message will become visible, as the writing will appear darker than the paper.

hello!

Wow!! it's back again!

Conclusion

When the ink is exposed to heat, such as under an iron or on a radiator, the acid in the lemon juice turns a different colour and becomes visible. Lemon juice is an organic substance, which means it's derived from living matter (a lemon tree). Many organic substances combine chemically with oxygen when heated — this is called oxidation. This usually turns them brown or black. Many other acids will work in the same way, such as vinegar or fruit juice.

Why don't **you** try writing a coded

Huh? I thought I'd cracked it — bah!

message in invisible ink? Two layers of security to crack! That'll be even harder to decode!

HOW TO WRITE YOUR NAME IN BENGALI, COOKIE-STYLE!

Materials

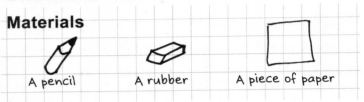

A pencil   A rubber   A piece of paper

Method

The Bengali alphabet has way more letters than the English alphabet, so to make it easy here are just a few Bengali letters that will help you write your name.

A	অ	H	র	O	অ
B	ব	I	২	P	প
C	ক	J	জ	R	র
D	ন	K	ক	S	স
E	এ	L	ল	T	ট
F	ফ	M	ম	U	অ
G	গ	N	ন	V	ভ

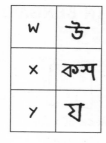

W	উ
X	ক্স
Y	য

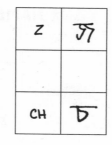

Z	স্য
CH	চ

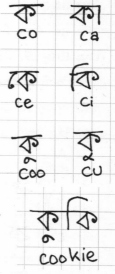

TH	ঠ
PH	ফ
SH	ষ

Each letter on its own acts as though it has a letter 'O' after it. So, the letter 'C' sounds like 'Co'. Just like we use vowels in English, in Bengali various symbols are added to letters to give them a sound.

ক co	কা ca
কে ce	কি ci
কু coo	কু cu

So, to write my name, I need to take the 'coo' sound and the 'ci' sound and put them together.

কুকি
cookie

See if you can write 'Vicky Chen' in Bengali. The answer is at the bottom of the page!

It may not be totally precise as I've not given you the whole alphabet, but see if you can write your own name now, or something close to it. Get a grown-up to check if you've done it right.

Answer: ভিকি চেন

253

Then see if you can decode the following words and names. The answers are upside down at the bottom of the page!

1. তিনা মিরুস
2. আক্সেল কান
3. মার্টিন
4. হাকা
5. ঠিকিন দিনা

Results

Different languages have different sounds. For instance, instead of using the letter 'Z', Bengali uses the letter 'J'.

Hi, I'm Kejiah

And I'm Jek

কেঠিঅম

ঠ্যক

Some of your names won't be totally precise, but that can happen in translation from different scripts.

Conclusion

You can now almost write in Bengali! A language is just like a code.

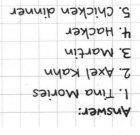

Answer:
1. Tina Movies
2. Axel Kahn
3. Martin
4. Hacker
5. Chicken dinner

Now that we've had a look at a few codes, if you're feeling extra brainy then why not try something a bit trickier using two layers of encryption?

We're going to use binary, like I saw at the Science Museum. If you remember, the binary system uses just 0s and 1s.

In order to write the number 1 in binary, you put a '1' in the '1' column.

Number	8	4	2	1	Binary
1				1	1

To write the number 2, you put a '0' in the '1' column and a '1' in the '2' column.

Number	8	4	2	1	Binary
1				1	1
2			1	0	10

To write the number 3, you put a '1' in the '1' column and a '1' in the '2' column, because 1 + 2 = 3.

Number	8	4	2	1	Binary
1				1	1
2			1	0	10
3			1	1	11

The columns are headed with numbers that double in value as you go along, starting with '1' at the right, then doubling to 2, 4, 8, 16, 32, 64 and so on.

Number	16	8	4	2	1	Binary
1	0	0	0	0	1	1
2	0	0	0	1	0	10
3	0	0	0	1	1	11
4	0	0	1	0	0	100
5	0	0	1	0	1	101
6	0	0	1	1	0	110
7	0	0	1	1	1	111
8	0	1	0	0	0	1000

So, to write the number 100, you write 1100100, because 64 + 32 + 4 = 100. There is no other way to write the number 100 using the binary system other than putting 1s and 0s in these columns. It's so clever.

Number	64	32	16	8	4	2	1	Binary
100	1	1	0	0	1	0	0	1100100

See if you can decode the message below. The answer is upside down at the bottom of the opposite page.

10111 ✳ 1001 ✳ 1110 ✳ 1110 ✳ 101 ✳ 10010
10111 ✳ 1001 ✳ 1110 ✳ 1110 ✳ 101 ✳ 10010
11 ✳ 1000 ✳ 1001 ✳ 11 ✳ 101 ✳ 1110
100 ✳ 1001 ✳ 1110 ✳ 1110 ✳ 101 ✳ 10010

First you will need to decode the binary numbers into actual numbers.

Then you'll need to turn the numbers into letters using this key.

If you know the key, then you can always decipher the code.

A	B	C	D	E	F	G	H	I	J	K	L	M
1	2	3	4	5	6	7	8	9	10	11	12	13

N	O	P	Q	R	S	T	U	V	W	X	Y	Z
14	15	16	17	18	19	20	21	22	23	24	25	26

Answer: Winner, Winner, Chicken Dinner

HOW TO MAKE YOUR OWN PAPER PLANE, COOKIE-STYLE!

Materials

A piece of paper

Coloured pens, colouring pencils, crayons, stickers – anything to decorate it with!

Method

Fold your piece of paper in half lengthways.

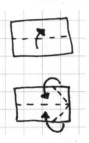

Fold in the two corners at one end so that they meet at the fold you've just made.

Fold the paper inwards again, so that edges A and B touch the centre fold.

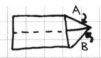

Now fold the whole thing in half.

 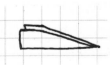

Then fold each wing down along the dotted line I've drawn here.

You should now have your very own paper aeroplane!

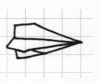

Finally, pinch the nose and angle it downwards a tiny bit to make your paper plane more aerodynamic.

Results

The paper's been folded in such a way that your plane should fly through the air.

Conclusion

The more aerodynamic a plane is, the less drag force it encounters so the quicker it will be. Drag force is the air resistance pushing back on a moving vehicle. The more streamlined a plane is, the faster it goes. So, the flatter and less bulky something is, the swifter it will travel, which is why a racing car is much faster than a bus.

Later, dude!

For anything to be still or travel at a constant speed, the forces acting on it need to be balanced.

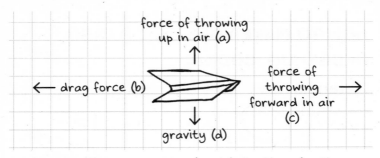

force of throwing
up in air (a)

← drag force (b)

force of
throwing
forward in air
(c) →

gravity (d)

When we throw a paper plane into the air, the force of throwing it up in the air (a) is greater than the force of gravity (d) and the force of throwing it forward (c) is greater than the drag force (or air resistance) pulling it back (b). As soon as the force of throwing it in the air becomes less than gravity, the plane starts to fall, and once the drag or air resistance is greater than the force of throwing it forward, it starts to slow down.

When (a) is greater than (b), the plane accelerates forwards. When (b) is greater than (a), the plane slows down.

a > b = accelerating plane
b > a = plane slows down

When (c) is greater than (d), the plane goes up. When (d) is greater than (c), the plane starts to fall.

c > d = plane goes up
d > c = plane falls down

HOW TO MAKE YOUR OWN MANGO HEDGEHOG, COOKIE-STYLE!

Materials

One mango  A knife

Method

Cut the mango in half and remove the stone.

Score each half with a criss-cross pattern.

Turn your mango inside out so the skin is flat on the bottom.

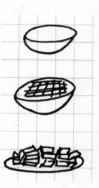

Results

Your mango now looks like a hedgehog!

And it's much easier to eat without getting a sticky mouth and fingers.

It looks nothing like me!

Conclusion

Yummy!

PRESS

Thank you for choosing a Piccadilly Press book.

If you would like to know more about our authors, our books or if you'd just like to know what we're up to, you can find us online.

www.piccadillypress.co.uk

And you can also find us on:

We hope to see you soon!